Get to know the girls of

BY
THALIA KALKIPSAKIS

ILLUSTRATED BY
ASH OSWALD

SQUARE
FISH

FEIWEL AND FRIENDS
NEW YORK

SQUARE FISH

An Imprint of Macmillan
175 Fifth Avenue
New York, NY 10010
mackids.com

Our books may be purchased in bulk for promotional, educational,
or business use. Please contact your local bookseller or the
Macmillan Corporate and Premium Sales Department
at (800) 221-7945 ext. 5442 or by e-mail at
MacmillanSpecialMarkets@macmillan.com.

Library of Congress Cataloging-in-Publication Data Available

ISBN 978-1-250-11262-0

First published in the United States by Feiwel and Friends
First U.S. Edition: 2008
Square Fish Reissue Edition: 2016
Square Fish logo designed by Filomena Tuosto

1   3   5   7   9   10   8   6   4   2

AR: 1.0

CHAPTER ONE

~Rosie's~ DANCE ACADEMY

Charlie looked up at the sign and grinned. Here she was at last—at a real dance school. No more dancing in the cold church basement. No more boring ballet classes with old Miss Plum.

Charlie was finally at a real school that taught modern dance.

She hitched her bag higher on her shoulder, took a deep breath, and pushed on the heavy old door.

She could already hear music pounding from the studio above. From the thudding and clapping, it sounded like a toddler class. Or maybe junior beginners.

For months, Charlie had begged her parents to let her start dancing here. At first, they had just said no. The classes cost a lot of money. And to get here, Charlie had to catch a bus all by herself.

But two weeks ago, as a birthday surprise, Charlie's parents had said yes.

Quietly, Charlie climbed up the stairs. Soon, she came to another door and another sign.

Charlie smiled to herself. Yet another thing that was different from her old ballet classes! This dance school was the real thing.

She was still smiling as she pushed open the second door.

But as she walked in and scanned the waiting area, Charlie gulped away her smile and felt her heart pounding quickly in her chest. Suddenly, the dance school seemed a long way from home.

Grouped in a huddle in the corner were four girls about Charlie's age. They were leaning in together as they giggled and whispered. From the backpacks near the group, Charlie could tell that they all went to the same school.

But they seemed linked in other ways, too—the way they sat with their legs crossed, the cut of their T-shirts. They even wore the same funky black dance shoes.

Charlie didn't even realize she was staring. But she couldn't take her eyes off their shoes. *Oh, no!* she thought. *The shoes.*

"Can I help you?" asked one of the girls, sitting up straight and looking at Charlie.

Her hair was long and worn loose like the others. She was smiling, but her eyes seemed cold.

"Ummm," Charlie looked down at her school shoes, wondering if she should just turn around and go home. "I'm OK," she mumbled.

For some reason, she wanted to hide from the group of girls. But the waiting area was not very big.

Charlie walked a few steps to the nearest wall. She wasn't thinking straight. All she could think of was hiding.

Then another girl walked up to Charlie. She had dark, curly hair that bounced when she moved. She wasn't from the group of friends, but she wore the same black dance shoes.

"Are you looking for the bathroom?" she said. She raised her eyebrows and gave Charlie a broad smile. "It's through there."

The next thing she knew, Charlie was turning the lock in a bathroom stall. Did she say thanks to that girl? She had wanted to. But she had felt too shy to talk.

Charlie leaned against the stall door and took a gulp of air.

Never mind. Charlie couldn't worry about saying thanks now. She had other things to worry about.

Charlie unzipped her bag and looked inside. For the past four years, she had worn the same clothes to dance class—a plain black leotard, pink tights, and pink ballet shoes. Yuk.

Why was Miss Plum so old-fashioned?

Charlie was so used to the old uniform that she hadn't thought of getting new clothes for this class.

Oh, no!
My clothes
are so
old-fashioned.

But she couldn't wear ballet shoes at a modern dance class. Could she?

Charlie shook her head and sighed. If she didn't wear her ballet shoes, what could she do? Her tights had feet in them. It would be too slippery to dance like that.

But if she didn't wear tights, what was she left with? Just a black leotard and bare legs. For some reason, that almost felt like dancing naked.

Charlie shook her head again and groaned. *How could this be happening?*

Not now!

Then she heard the thud and bang of the beginners coming out of the dance studio.

Charlie's first class in modern dance was about to start.

CHAPTER
TWO

"Scissors? What do you want scissors for?"

The receptionist frowned over the counter at Charlie. She had long hair, worn loose, like everyone else.

"I . . . um . . . " Charlie didn't know what to say. She couldn't tell the receptionist what she was planning.

"You're the new girl, aren't you?" the receptionist said. But she wasn't smiling.

Charlie nodded. She could hear whispering and giggles as the girls walked behind her and into the studio.

"Make sure you bring them back," the receptionist said. Then her voice softened. "OK?"

"OK, thanks."

Charlie took the scissors and rushed back into the bathroom.

She had to work fast.

As she snipped, she thought about what her mom was going to say. But Charlie couldn't worry about that now.

Making Mom mad was better than wearing ballet shoes to a modern dance class. There was no way Charlie was going

to do that. Not in front of those trendy girls. She just couldn't!

As she stepped into her leotard, Charlie thought about taking her hair out of its ponytail and pulling off her headband. But she didn't have time to fuss with her hair. She was already late for class.

Charlie put everything except the scissors back in her bag.

She took a deep breath. This was it.

Time to face the music.

"Weeeeeeeelcome, Charlie!" Rosie, the dance teacher, yelled above the music. As she clapped her hands, her nail polish glittered. "Just find a spot at the barre."

The rest of the class stopped kicking and stared at Charlie.

Charlie could feel all eyes on her, looking at her ponytail and her plain black leotard. Under that, she wore pink tights, cut off at the knees, and below that, bare feet. She felt her cheeks burning as she clutched the barre. She wished she could disappear. It was like being naked in front of a mob of cameras.

"OK, warm up, girls."

Rosie changed the music and started counting in time.

The rest of the class stopped staring, and started kicking and stretching at the barre.

"Just copy the others, Charlie," Rosie called. "You'll be fine!"

And for most of the class, Charlie *was* fine.

Once everyone started working and stretching together, Charlie stopped feeling quite so different.

She was surprised how similar this warm-up was to her old ballet warm-up. The kicks and stretches weren't too hard at all.

The leaps across the floor were fine, too. It was pretty much the same as ballet, except the rhythm was different. When the other girls leaped across the floor, they reminded Charlie of deer—leaping with strength and power.

But when it was Charlie's turn, she felt

light and pale. She didn't know how to stop leaping like a ballet dancer.

The girl who had shown Charlie the bathroom was easily the best dancer. Her name was Kathy, and she had a dynamic, punchy way of moving. She was balanced on the floor, but she seemed to fly through each leap.

Charlie couldn't stop watching her.

Kathy is an amazing dancer!

The way Kathy moved was exactly why Charlie wanted to learn modern dance.

But then it came time to dance in the middle of the floor.

As soon as they started a dance sequence, Charlie realized that modern dance was very different from ballet.

Everything was so fast. The other girls seemed to explode out of themselves, kicking, spinning, ducking. They all had a special way of flicking their heads to the side with a rush of long hair.

Charlie fumbled and faked it for a while.

Then she just stood at the back of the room, wondering how on earth she could ever dance like that.

"Don't worry, Charlie," Rosie called out. "We've been practicing this for weeks."

Some of the girls turned and sniggered.

But Kathy didn't. She moved in front of Charlie and slowly went through the moves. Charlie smiled a thanks, and tried to copy Kathy.

But it was no use. Charlie just couldn't get into the flow. She felt so out of place —she didn't belong here at all.

Charlie had not expected modern dance to be easy, but she also hadn't expected to feel like this—so very new and so utterly, completely different.

CHAPTER THREE

"Charlotte Anderson, what on *earth?*"

Charlie's mom stood in the doorway of her bedroom, frowning. She held up Charlie's ballet tights with the feet cut out.

"Oh . . . yeah . . ." Charlie jumped up from her bed, letting the magazine she was reading drop to the floor. "I *had* to cut the feet out." Charlie cleared her throat. "I couldn't wear my ballet shoes."

"Hmmm," said Charlie's mom, shaking her head. But she didn't seem too angry. "Imagine what Miss Plum would say if she saw these tights!" Her eyes twinkled.

Charlie giggled. Now was the time to ask her mom something.

"Mom—"

Just then, Charlie's brother yelled out from his bedroom. "Moooooomm, where's my *soccer jersey?*"

Charlie's mom yelled right back at him. "It's in the *dryer*, Harry."

"Awwww, Mom!" Harry's voice came back.

There was always a lot of yelling at Charlie's house. Not because anyone was angry. That was just how everyone talked to each other.

But not Charlie. She preferred to stay quiet, or to speak face-to-face.

It was the same at school. Charlie didn't say much there, either. The only person she really talked to was her best friend, Laura. Laura wanted to be a singer and she understood Charlie better than anyone.

Now Charlie tried to make her voice loud for once. "Mom, I need new dance shoes."

"Oh, Charlotte," her mom said, shaking her head.

"All the girls wear them," Charlie said. "Pleeeeease, Mom?"

Her mom leaned down and put her hands on Charlie's shoulders. "Charlotte, you just started," she said.

Charlie nodded.

"So let's make sure you like the new classes first, OK?"

Pleeeeease, Mom?

Charlie sighed. Of course she liked them. It was just all so different from what she had imagined, that's all.

"My little butterfly!" Charlie's mom winked. "Maybe ballet suits you better, after all." She kissed Charlie on the forehead and walked out of the room.

Charlie slumped back on her bed.

A butterfly.

Her mom always called her that.

But Charlie didn't want to be a butterfly. She wanted to be able to dance strong and fast, like the rest of the class.

At the start of the next class, Charlie was feeling good. She told herself not to worry about the shoes. And this time, she didn't feel quite so out of place.

She was wearing new dancing tights that she had bought with her allowance. They were black and cut off above the knees. Over those, Charlie wore her swimsuit from last summer. It was a trendy lime green—perfect, except the straps were a bit thin.

Over the top, she wore an old black T-shirt—cut to look like a dance top, of course!

Charlie was getting pretty handy with a pair of scissors.

At the start of the class, Kathy called Charlie over to a spot at the barre. They stretched together while Kathy talked

about her gymnastics team. It sounded like a lot of work. No wonder Kathy's dancing was so good.

"Gymnastics is really hard," Kathy said, from upside down in a stretch. She looked up and smiled at Charlie. "It's not as much fun as dancing."

"OK, girls!" Rosie called out. "We need to talk about the recital."

"Yay!" Kathy whispered.

Charlie raised her eyebrows. She hadn't expected a recital!

Everyone stretched quietly while Rosie talked. The recital was only two months away, and Rosie wanted to spend more time practicing.

When Rosie said that, the trendy girls started whispering together. Even Kathy looked excited.

Then Rosie walked over to Charlie at the barre. She leaned in close enough for Charlie to see her sparkling orange nails.

"It's a little late to fit you into our dance, Charlie," Rosie said.

Charlie pulled out of her stretch and nodded shyly. She used to love her old ballet recitals. But she couldn't imagine doing a modern dance onstage!

"But I still want you to be an understudy," Rosie said, smiling. "If someone gets sick, then you dance in their place, OK?"

"Ummm . . ." Charlie wasn't sure about that. *What if someone did get sick?*

"Just watch for the first run-through," Rosie called back, as she walked over to the CD player. "Then you can copy the others!"

Kathy winked at Charlie. "Don't worry, I'll help you," she said.

Charlie just gulped.

CHAPTER FOUR

"Places, everyone!" cried Rosie.

It was time to practice the dance for the recital. But Charlie was still at the barre, stunned that she was now an understudy.

Please, don't let anyone get sick, she thought.

The rest of the class formed an excited line at the back of the room. Charlie slipped quietly around to watch from the front.

Then the music started—loud and strong, with a pulsing beat.

Boom, boom, boom.

With the beat of the music, the line of dancers started moving jerkily like a machine. Their legs were stiff. Their arms moved like cogs in a machine.

Thud, thud, clunk.

Charlie sat down and hugged her knees. The dancers were so clever. They looked just like robots!

Soon, the music changed. The clunking sounds stopped and a sweet voice started singing.

Friday night and the lights are low . . .

Now, one of the dancers broke away

from the machine. It was Kathy. She danced in the center of the room, with the other dancers still clunking like robots behind her.

Her body seemed to move exactly how the singer sounded—groovy and happy.

This dance is fantastic!

Now Charlie recognized the music. It was called "Dancing Queen," and it was the same music from the last class.

As the music quickened, Kathy's dancing got faster and more dynamic until she was leaping across the room with joy. She even started doing gymnastic flips.

Next, Kathy ran to the dancing machine, pulling the other girls' arms, and urging the robots to dance.

One by one, each of the girls broke away from the machine until, finally, the whole class was dancing together, funky and free.

You are the Dancing Queen . . .

It was the same dance sequence that Charlie had faked her way through last week. But it made sense now. Of course it was fast—it had to be. That was part of the story.

As soon as the dance finished, Rosie asked them all to start again.

This time, Charlie moved to the side of the room and copied the others. As they danced, Rosie called out instructions to the class.

"Robots, eyes on the floor."

"Shoulders down, Kathy. Good!"

"Smile, girls! You're supposed to be happy now."

By the end of the class, Charlie was buzzing. She had only managed to pick up some of the dance. But that didn't matter.

She was determined to learn the dance the right way.

The dance for the recital was fabulous!

But as Charlie pulled on her clothes in the waiting area after class, one of the trendy girls called out to her.

"What are you up to now, Charlie?"

"Oh, um . . ." Charlie looked down at her feet. *Was the girl being nice to her?*

"Looks like you're going swimming!" the girl said in a nasty voice.

One of her friends laughed. Another friend hit the first girl on the arm.

Charlie felt blood rushing to her cheeks and a lump form in her throat. She wanted to run away and hide again.

"I like your bathing suit, Charlie," Kathy said, pulling on a sweater and smiling. Her curly hair bounced on her shoulders. "That color is cool!"

"Yeah, don't worry about me, Charlie," said the trendy girl. "I was only teasing."

She said it like it was a good thing. Then she made a hissing noise and scratched her hand in the air like a cat.

The others did the same, and laughed.

They seemed to have forgotten about Charlie and Kathy.

Kathy rolled her big eyes. "I'll walk you downstairs," she said.

Charlie walked with Kathy in silence down the stairs. The shrieks and laughter of the trendy girls filtered down to them.

When Charlie said bye to Kathy, she tried to smile, but she didn't really feel like it. Kathy was nice. But Charlie didn't like the other girls.

Being new wasn't just about dancing, it was about fitting in. But nothing Charlie did seemed good enough for the trendy girls.

CHAPTER FIVE

"You are the Dancing Queen," Laura's voice sang out among the trees as Charlie practiced the dance at school.

There was a spot, right behind the pine tree area, that was almost hidden from view. It was the only place where Charlie didn't feel too shy to dance at school.

Sometimes, someone would run past

playing tag, but usually the other kids didn't go near them.

As Charlie danced, the dry pine needles kicked up around her feet.

Kick and lean back . . . swivel on two feet . . .

Charlie was getting used to the speed of the dance now. She had been practicing for weeks. At night, she would pull open the curtains in the living room, and use the windows as mirrors.

She must have done the dance a hundred times by now!

In fact, she had practiced so many times that it didn't even feel fast anymore. The dance just felt happy and free.

Sometimes, Charlie even felt like she

had time within the dance to reach out a little further or to kick a little higher.

Time, even, to dream that *she* was the Dancing Queen.

As Laura hummed the end of the song, Charlie leapt to the side of her pretend stage for the end of the dance.

"Yay, Charlie!" Laura clapped. "You make it look easy."

Charlie smiled and shrugged.

The dancing was easier now. In fact, her old ballet training had come in handy. But she still didn't feel like she fit in at the new dance school.

"Bet you're the best in the class," Laura said.

Charlie let out a small laugh and shook her head.

Then Laura started singing again.

"Charlie's the Dancing Queen, shy and sweet, see her tiny feet!"

They both laughed and sat down on the roots of a tall pine tree.

"I'll never be the best in the class," Charlie said after a while.

"Yeah, right!" Laura started pushing pine needles into a big pile.

"I'm not . . ." Charlie searched for the right words. "I'm too . . . *different*."

Laura shifted over so that she was sitting on her pile of pine needles like it was a cushion.

"That's just because you're new," Laura said. She started pushing more pine needles into a new pile.

Charlie shrugged. She wasn't so new anymore. The trendy girls didn't tease Charlie now, not like that time with the swimsuit. But they still weren't very nice to her, either.

They never said hello or bye to Charlie. They were always too busy giggling and whispering in a group.

When Charlie finally came to class wearing real dance shoes, the trendy girls didn't even notice!

She didn't have any idea how to make them like her. She still didn't know how to fit in.

But after weeks of classes at the new dance school, Charlie did know one thing.

She knew that she loved to dance.

"Your throne, my lady," Laura said in a posh voice. She pointed at a new pile of pine needles.

Charlie giggled.

Then she sat on her throne, laughing and pretending to be a queen.

CHAPTER SIX

Charlie sat under the barre and hugged her knees.

The new costumes glittered and shimmered as the rest of the class held them up with *ooohs* and *aaahs*.

Charlie sighed quietly. There was no costume for Charlie. She wasn't in the recital, so she didn't need one.

"Put it around your neck like this,"

Rosie said, showing the class how to put on their costumes.

As Charlie watched, the rest of the class tried their costumes on. They looked like shiny metal robots.

Charlie sighed again.

When she had first heard about the recital, she had been scared stiff. But that felt like a long time ago. Now that she knew the dance so well, Charlie thought she could dance onstage if she had to.

In fact, maybe wearing the costume and dancing onstage would be fun.

"When you break away from the machine," Rosie said, "you do this." She pulled at the Velcro on Kathy's costume.

As the silver material came away, Rosie pulled it in a glittering circle. Then she wrapped it around Kathy's waist to make a shimmery skirt.

It glittered and rippled over Kathy's hips as she moved.

"Ooooooh!" said everyone.

The rest of the class copied. Soon, they were all standing together in sparkling dancing skirts.

Charlie rested her chin on her knees. She wanted to reach out and touch the shiny skirts.

"OK, OK!" Rosie clapped her hands. "Costumes off while we warm up."

"Awww!" the girls groaned.

"You can put them back on after that," Rosie said, smiling.

When it happened, Charlie was in another world.

In her mind, she was a clunking robot, stuck in a machine and forced to do the same work day after day.

It didn't matter that she was dancing to the side, away from the rest of the class. It didn't even matter that she wasn't wearing a costume.

In her mind, Charlie was a robot, about to break away from the machine and be free. When Kathy broke away, Charlie kept jolting and jerking like the others.

That was when it happened.

Kathy was smiling, broad and big as always. She pulled the costume from around her neck and wrapped it around her waist. She twirled and leapt with the skirt flowing around her.

Then Kathy jumped back into one flip, and then another. . . .

But this time, as Kathy flipped back, the new skirt got caught under her hands. As Kathy pushed off, her hands slipped on the skirt.

With a cry, Kathy crashed awkwardly to the floor.

It took Charlie a while to come out of her daydream and realize what had happened. But when she did, she felt sick watching.

Kathy was groaning and sobbing while Rosie put an ice pack on her ankle.

Before long, Rosie had carried Kathy out into the waiting area.

Soon, everyone heard the receptionist talking on the phone to Kathy's mom.

". . . You should probably take Kathy to the hospital."

Charlie gulped and shook her head.

Not Kathy.

And not now! It was only three weeks until the recital.

The trendy girls were whispering in a group. But they seemed more excited than worried.

Charlie glanced at the rest of the class. Then she tiptoed to the waiting area and peeked around the door.

Kathy was lying on the floor with her ankle propped up on a chair. Her cheeks and hair were wet with tears. Rosie and the receptionist were talking quickly in another room.

Poor Kathy! Charlie knelt on the floor beside her friend.

"Oh Kathy, don't cry," Charlie whispered. "It'll be all right."

Kathy took a quivering breath. "I'm going to miss the recital. . . ."

Charlie shook her head. But she knew Kathy was right.

". . . *and* level tests at gymnastics!" Kathy continued.

Then she started crying again.

Charlie held her friend's hand, wishing she knew what to say.

After a while, Kathy took a big gulp of air.

"At least you'll have a spot in the dance," Kathy said, trying to smile. "That's one good thing."

Charlie shook her head again. She still didn't know what to say.

Being in the recital and wearing the costume would be wonderful. But she didn't want Kathy to miss out.

Right now, Charlie didn't know what to hope for.

CHAPTER
SEVEN

When Kathy had left for the hospital, Rosie walked back into the studio, frowning.

The whole class watched as she walked to the CD player and tapped her fingernails on the lid.

Rat-a-tat-tat. Rat-a-tat-tat.

Everyone was quiet, watching.

"Well!" Rosie tried to smile, but her eyes looked worried. "Change of plans."

Charlie held her breath.

Rosie walked around from behind the CD player and stood in front of the class.

She looked at Charlie.

"Lucky we have an understudy," Rosie said.

Charlie nodded but she didn't smile. It all seemed so serious. And something else was worrying her.

Right away one of the trendy girls said out loud what was worrying Charlie.

"But what about Kathy's solo?"

The whole class looked up at Rosie. *What about Kathy's solo?*

"Well, there's not much time, but we'll have to hold an audition." Rosie scanned the girls in the class. "I want you all to try out for the part of the Dancing Queen."

Until now, everyone had been quiet. But suddenly everyone—everyone except Charlie—started talking at once.

"But how can we?"

"Kathy's solo has all those flippy things in it!"

I can't replace Kathy.

"We can't do that!"

Rosie yelled above the noise and clapped her hands in a glitter of nail polish.

"OK, OK!" Rosie yelled.

When the room was quiet, she continued talking.

"Now, girls. Our dance isn't about flips." Rosie put her hands on her hips. "Can anyone tell me what our dance *is* about?"

Everyone was quiet.

"Being happy?" someone said, after a while.

"Dancing with your friends?" said someone else.

Charlie hugged her knees and looked at her dancing shoes. She loved the dance.

For her, doing the dance was like living a perfect dream.

"Well, for me," said Rosie, "the dance is about being yourself. The Dancing Queen breaks away from the crowd and dances her own special dance."

Rosie smiled at the class.

"Next week, I want you all to show me your own special dance. Whatever that is. It doesn't have to have flips."

Rosie smiled at Charlie. "You, too, Charlie," Rosie said. "I want *everyone* to try out. Show me the dance that comes from your heart."

When Rosie said that, everyone started talking again.

Charlie kept hugging her knees, but she couldn't help smiling. In just one class, everything had changed so much. Now she didn't just have a spot in the dance, she was also allowed to try out for the main part!

After class that night, Charlie pulled open the curtains in the living room so she could see herself in the windows.

Her mom's voice floated in from the kitchen. "You are the Daaancing Queeeen . . ."

Charlie's mom wasn't a very good singer. She sounded like an opera singer with a sore throat. But it was nice of her to be excited for Charlie.

When Charlie had told her mom that she was going to be in the recital, Charlie's mom had given her a bear hug.

"Lucky we bought those dancing shoes!" she had said.

But now Charlie had more than dancing shoes to worry about.

Keeping an eye on her reflection in the window, Charlie danced through Kathy's solo. She had watched Kathy do it so many times that she already knew it by heart.

In the parts where Kathy did her gymnastic flips, Charlie worked out some leaps and turns to do instead. But she still felt like a butterfly, just like her mom had said.

She could tell she wasn't half as good as Kathy. The punchy, bold parts looked so good when Kathy did them. But Charlie didn't feel at all like a queen when she tried to copy. She felt weak and silly.

Charlie flopped down on the carpet and made a face at the window.

What was the point? Rosie would never pick Charlie to be the Dancing Queen. She was the newest in the class, after all.

But until Rosie picked someone else next week, Charlie could dream.

CHAPTER EIGHT

"When is it? I'll have to come!"

At school the next day, Laura gave Charlie a hug. She seemed even more excited about the recital than Charlie.

"But there's more," Charlie said over Laura's shoulder.

Laura pulled away from the hug to look at her. "More?"

"Kathy was the Dancing Queen. . . ."

Charlie trailed off. *Poor Kathy.* She must be so disappointed. "So we all get to try out for her part."

"Oooooo!" Laura's eyes were wide. "They'll pick you for sure!"

Charlie laughed and shook her head. "I knew you would say that, Laura!"

"Well, it's true," Laura said, grinning. "You keep saying how differently you dance."

The bell rang and they both picked up their bags.

"That's what the dance is about, isn't it?" Laura said. "Being different?"

Charlie just shrugged.

But for the rest of the day, she kept thinking about the part of the Dancing

Queen. Laura's words had given Charlie an idea.

Maybe being different wasn't so bad after all.

After school, Charlie was back in the living room at home. She put "Dancing Queen" on the CD player and pressed repeat.

Then she stood in the center of the room, listening and swaying to the music.

But this time, Charlie didn't worry about Kathy's solo or her gymnastic flips. She didn't worry about trying to fit in.

She didn't even worry about what she looked like in the window.

Charlie listened to the sweet voice and shut her eyes. She let the tune and rhythm settle inside.

As she swayed to the music, Charlie thought about everything that had happened to her.

Begging her parents to let her start at the new dance school.

Hiding from the trendy girls on her first day.

Trying to dance like the others and feeling weak, like a butterfly.

Charlie let it all flow through her— feeling so different, learning so much and now loving how the dance made her feel.

Then Charlie started to dance.

As she moved, all her feelings seemed
to flow out through her body.

you are the Dancing Queen

It was like the words hiding inside were now coming out as she danced. Reaching to the side felt like it was for hope and yearning. Charlie pulled in for sadness, and hid safe in her own arms.

Then she leapt in joy.

The soft flow of an arm movement felt like a peaceful dream. Charlie leaned back, feeling shy, and then exploded out, just because she was alive.

Slowly, section by section, Charlie felt her way through her new dance. Each time she went through it, she relived everything through her body. It was like dancing in her own, private world.

When she was finished, Charlie felt

clear and calm. She felt happy.

And feeling the way she did, Charlie stopped worrying about being picked to be the Dancing Queen. Right now, she felt too good to worry about that.

The story of the Dancing Queen became Charlie's story about being different, and fitting in. After being so shy and scared, Charlie felt like she had finally found her voice.

CHAPTER nine

For the rest of the week, Charlie felt calm. Even when she wasn't practicing her dance, she still felt different, like she was holding a smile in her heart.

Whenever she had a chance, Charlie practiced her solo—changing moves here and adding an extra flourish there.

She even tried leaving her hair loose and flipping it around like the rest of the class. But in the end, Charlie tied her hair back into a ponytail. It felt better that way.

Over the weekend, Charlie called her mom into the living room to show her the new dance.

At first, Charlie's mom kept flipping through her address book, only half watching Charlie.

But as Charlie kept dancing, her mom put the address book down. Soon a funny, surprised look came over her mom's face.

When Charlie finished her solo, her mom was quiet, staring at Charlie with the same surprised look on her face.

"What's wrong, Mom?" asked Charlie. "Don't you like it?"

"Oh, Charlotte," her mom shook her head in wonder. "It's beautiful."

At school, Laura started calling Charlie the Dancing Queen, and told everyone about the audition. When the teacher wished Charlie luck, everyone stared at her. But she held the calm feeling in her heart and didn't feel like blushing at all.

Charlie felt happy right until the next dance class—the audition.

As she walked up the stairs to the dance school, she even felt excited about showing everyone her solo. Maybe Rosie would like Charlie's dance as much as her mom did.

But then, as she opened the door, Charlie saw the trendy girls. They were wearing their costumes, and had ultra-stylish hair. One of them was even wearing makeup.

The other girls look so stylish.

As Charlie walked past them, she felt the calmness trickle away and disappear, like it was hiding out of reach. With that came the rush of worries—wondering what the trendy girls would think, and fretting that she didn't have a costume.

She wondered why she had bothered to come today at all. Rosie would never pick her for the main part!

All through the auditions, Charlie sat in a corner, hugging her knees.

She could tell that the trendy girls had been practicing together. Their solos were a lot like Kathy's. And in the parts they had changed, all four did the same head flips and hip rocks.

Finally, everyone except Charlie had had her turn.

"OK Charlie, best for last!" Rosie called.

Charlie stood up and ducked under the barre. As she walked to the center of the room, her heart pounded in her chest—

stronger than ever before. She felt all eyes on her—no costume, her cheeks red.

Silly Charlie.

The music started and the sweet voice began to sing.

Friday night and the lights are low . . .

But Charlie couldn't move. It felt like the voice was singing for someone else, someone like the trendy girls. It didn't feel like the song was for Charlie anymore.

Charlie shut her eyes and tried to hold the voice inside like before. But all she could feel was the thudding of her heart.

Suddenly, the music stopped.

"What's wrong, Charlie?" Rosie asked kindly.

Charlie shook her head.

She could hardly breathe, let alone talk.

"I . . . I *can't*," Charlie said.

One of the trendy girls whispered something to the others.

Charlie shook her head again. "I don't want to. . . ."

But she felt like crying when she heard her own words.

Rosie was quiet for a while, tapping the lid of the CD player.

Then she nodded.

"OK, girls. I'll give you the answer next week," she said.

In a fog, Charlie went and sat with the rest of the class. She wished she were someone else, like the trendy girls— always happy and never scared.

Life would be so much better that way.

CHAPTER TEN

At the end of the class, Rosie called Charlie over to talk.

"Kathy's mom is going to drop by with her costume this week," Rosie said.

Charlie nodded down at her shoes. She hated herself for being so shy.

"How is Kathy?" Charlie asked quietly.

"She's OK, poor thing," Rosie said. "She's coming to watch the recital."

Charlie managed to look up at Rosie and smile.

But Rosie looked thoughtful. "Why don't you show me your solo now?" she said. "I'd love to see it."

"Oh," Charlie glanced out the door to the waiting area. She could hear the rest of the class talking and laughing together.

"Hang on." Rosie ran over and shut the door. Then she gently led Charlie by the shoulders to the center of the room. "Just dance for me," Rosie said. "OK?"

Charlie wanted to shake her head. Then the music started.

Friday night and the lights are low . . .

Somehow, with the other girls out of

the room, Charlie felt the sweet voice reaching inside her like before.

Before she could think, Charlie was dancing. But not just dancing—she was feeling it all inside, coming from her heart. The hope and fear and joy all came out as Charlie danced for her teacher just like when she danced at home.

When Charlie had finished, Rosie smiled and nodded.

"See you next week," she said.

Everyone was stunned.

The whole class stared at Rosie with

mouths open and eyes wide.

It was the week after the audition, less than one week until the recital.

Charlie couldn't see her own face, but she knew that she must have looked more stunned than anyone.

What did Rosie just say?

"Me?" she stammered. "I—"

Her heart was pounding again, but not like last week. Part of her felt good. She was surprised and scared, but also happy. *Thrilled.*

"I know you had a case of stage fright last week," Rosie said. "But I'm sure you can do it, Charlie."

The trendy girls were whispering to each other as they looked at Charlie.

Charlie shook her head. "I can't," she said. *Not with everyone watching,* she thought.

"Here," Rosie said kindly. She gave Charlie a bag. "Just put on Kathy's costume and give it a go."

Charlie nodded and ran to the bathroom. She was glad to escape from the eyes of the rest of the class.

Once she was safely inside the bath-

room stall, Charlie put her hand over her mouth and laughed out loud.

She couldn't believe it! Rosie had asked her to be the Dancing Queen!

She couldn't imagine doing her dance in front of the trendy girls, and definitely not at the recital!

But it still felt great to be asked.

Charlie pulled the shimmery costume out of the bag and carefully pulled it on.

It felt fantastic.

She leaned back, all glittery, against the door. Then she took a long, deep breath.

Rosie must have thought Charlie's solo was good. But was it good enough to dance in the recital?

What if she had stage fright again?

Charlie took another breath and shook her head. No, she was too shy to dance her solo for the recital. She would have to tell Rosie to choose someone else.

Charlie picked up the empty bag, ready to go back and talk to Rosie.

But then she stopped.

The bag wasn't empty.

At the bottom of the bag was a small package with Charlie's name on it.

Inside was a delicate plastic butterfly. Its wings were white and shimmery.

She peered at the delicate wings, smiling. They reminded her of something. . . .

Then she noticed a note tucked into the wrapping.

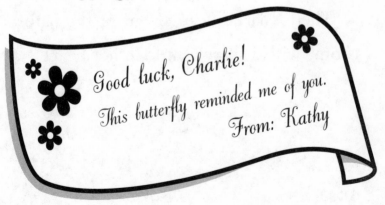

Good luck, Charlie!
This butterfly reminded me of you.
From: Kathy

Charlie smiled at the note. Kathy was so kind. Right from the start, she had been nice to Charlie. She didn't care that Charlie was different.

Why then, did Charlie worry about the trendy girls? It didn't matter what they thought. Charlie already had a friend in the class. A *good* friend. After a while, she tucked the butterfly and note safely back in the bag.

Then Charlie headed out of the bathroom, with a secret smile in her heart.

CHAPTER ELEVEN

It was very dark. Charlie heard a cough from the audience, then the shuffling of feet as she and her class ran onto the stage.

Together, they formed a human machine. Arms linked, bodies close, all of them waiting as one.

Charlie could feel the familiar pounding in her chest. But she could also feel something else inside—another feeling that she knew quite well.

Then the music started, pounding through the theater.

Boom, boom, boom.

With it came the flashing strobe light and the clunking of the machine.

Charlie jerked her arms in time with the others. Right now, she looked like them, and moved like them. She could even sense that she felt like them.

But she wasn't exactly the same.

As the music kept thudding, Charlie could feel her class tensing around her. They all knew what came next.

For a moment, Charlie's mind went blank and time seemed to stand still.

Then the flashing light stopped and the music changed. The whole theater seemed to hold its breath.

As the sweet voice rang out, Charlie felt it touch her inside.

Friday night and the lights are low . . .

With all eyes on her, Charlie pulled the costume from around her neck and wrapped it around her waist.

Then she was dancing. She twirled and leaped, kicked and reached.

Charlie still couldn't see the audience, but she knew they were all there—Kathy, Laura, her family. Even Miss Plum was there. They had all come to see Charlie dance.

But she wasn't just dancing for them. She was also dancing because she loved it. She felt like a butterfly flitting in the sunlight and, right now, that felt wonderful.

As the lights shone stronger, Charlie moved to the machine. She pulled at the

girls' arms, urging them to break away and be free. From the looks on their faces, Charlie could understand how the other girls felt—funky and fabulous.

Soon, the whole class was dancing together in the middle of the stage.

Then, too soon, it came time to leap offstage for the ending.

In an instant, the theater roared to life with claps and cheers. Charlie even heard a whooping sound from her brother.

But the class was in another world.

Together, they ran out of the wings, giggling and shushing each other in the corridor and then laughing and hugging in the dressing room.

Charlie even hugged the trendy girls.

"Charlie, how did you do it?" one of them asked. "I would have been scared stiff."

Charlie laughed. "I *was* scared stiff!"

Then they hugged and laughed again.

After the recital, Charlie and her class changed back into their normal clothes again. Everyone was still flushed with excitement. Plus, they only had a short break until the start of the next recital, when they would have to dance all over again.

"We're heading to the café for some food," one of the trendy girls called out.

"Who wants to come?"

Some of the other girls picked up their purses and headed for the door.

Charlie managed to look the trendy girl in the eye. "No thanks, Holly."

It felt good calling her by name.

She was, after all, a normal person.

"Maybe next time?" Charlie asked.

"OK," Holly nodded and smiled. Then she headed out the door with the others.

Charlie sat down on the dressing room floor and looked around. It felt good to be alone. But Charlie didn't want to hide in here.

She wanted to go outside and see her family, and Laura, and to say hi to Miss Plum.

But most of all, Charlie wanted to find Kathy. She had something to give her.

Charlie pulled it carefully from the corner of her makeup bag. It was a statue of a deer in the middle of a leap. It looked graceful and powerful, exactly like Kathy.

Charlie didn't have a note for Kathy, but she hoped Kathy would understand. The right present can say a lot.

After all, two people can still be friends, even if they both dance completely different.

THE END

BY
ROWAN McAULEY

ILLUSTRATED BY
ASH OSWALD

SQUARE
FISH

FEIWEL AND FRIENDS
NEW YORK

SQUARE
FISH

An Imprint of Macmillan
175 Fifth Avenue
New York, NY 10010
mackids.com

Our books may be purchased in bulk for promotional,
educational, or business use. Please contact your local
bookseller or the Macmillan Corporate and Premium Sales
Department at (800) 221-7945 ext. 5442 or by e-mail at
MacmillanSpecialMarkets@macmillan.com.

Library of Congress Cataloging-in-Publication Data Available

ISBN 978-1-250-11262-0

First published in Australia by E2,
an imprint of Hardie Grant Egmont.
Illustration and design by Ash Oswald.

First published in the United States by Feiwel and Friends
First Square Fish Edition: 2013
Square Fish Reissue Edition: 2016
Square Fish logo designed by Filomena Tuosto

1   3   5   7   9   10   8   6   4   2

AR: 3.9

CHAPTER ONE

It was six o'clock on Friday morning, the last day of school for the year. The alarm hadn't gone off yet, but Olivia was already awake, dressed, and sitting at the kitchen table, eating her toast and waiting for her mom to get up.

She drank a glass of milk and ate an apple, but her mom still slept on. She brushed her teeth and made her lunch, but even then her mom did not stir.

Olivia checked the clock on the microwave. Six thirty. Surely her mom should be awake by now? She tiptoed along the hallway and looked in. Her mom was fast asleep, snoring slightly. Olivia knocked gently on the open door. Her mom did not move.

Olivia cleared her throat, "Ahem!"

Her mom rolled over in bed and snored more loudly. Olivia was getting desperate.

"Mom," she whispered.

"Mom," she said gently.

"Mom!" she said more firmly.

This was getting her nowhere.

"MOM!" she yelled suddenly and stamped her foot.

"Hmm?" said her mom, sitting up in bed, her hair all fluffy on one side. "What's up, baby?"

"Mom," said Olivia. "You have to get up. I am sleeping over at Ching Ching's house tonight."

"Are you?" said her mom. "Are you sure? Did we talk about this?"

"Mom," said Olivia sternly, because she had to be strict with her mom sometimes. "You know it is. We talked about it on Monday, remember? You spoke with Mrs. Adams on the phone."

"I know, baby," said her mom,

yawning. "I'm just teasing you."

"Well," said Olivia, "will you get up now?"

"Mmm," said her mom, still sounding tired. "What time is it?"

"Six thirty," said Olivia. "Or even later by now. We've been talking for at least five minutes."

"Six thirty?"

"Or six thirty-five," said Olivia.

"Is the sun even up yet?" asked her mom.

"Mom!"

"OK, OK," said her mom. "I'm getting up. Even though it's still the middle of the night," she grumbled.

"Come on," said Olivia. "Here's your bathrobe."

Hurry UP, Mom, I'll be late!

While her mom took a shower, Olivia checked her bag again. As well as her lunchbox, she had packed her pajamas, her swimsuit, some clean clothes for tomorrow, her hairbrush, and a small box of chocolates for Ching Ching's mom, to say thank you. Was that everything?

It was almost seven o'clock and Olivia was dancing with impatience, waiting for her mom to finish blow-drying her hair. Finally, she was ready.

"OK," she said to Olivia. "Now, are you sure you have packed everything you need?"

"Yes," said Olivia.

"Pajamas?"

"Yes," said Olivia.

"Chocolates for Mrs. Adams?"

"Yes," said Olivia.

"Clean underwear for tomorrow?"

"Mom!"

"Well, have you?"

"YES!" said Olivia. "Come on!"

"All right!" said her mom. "Just checking.

I'll just get the keys. . . . "

But Olivia was already out the door and waiting at the front gate, her backpack on her back. Her mom locked the door and walked down the path (so slowly!), and together they walked to the bus stop.

"I'm going to miss you tonight," said her mom.

"Yeah, yeah," said Olivia, looking ahead for the bus.

"I will. I won't see you all day, I won't have anyone to eat dinner with, and you'll be at Ching Ching's until tomorrow. . . . "

"I know," said Olivia.

"What time am I picking you up?"

"Lunchtime," said Olivia. "Ching Ching

and I will have breakfast together, and play in the morning, and then you can pick me up at lunchtime."

"Lunchtime it is," said her mom, giving her a hug and a big smoochy kiss.

The bus was just arriving at the corner.

"Bye, mom," said Olivia, yelling back over her shoulder as she ran to catch it.

At last she was on her way.

CHAPTER TWO

On the bus, Olivia tried to relax. She looked out the window and noticed how few cars there were on the road. She looked around the bus and saw all the empty seats. She wasn't going to be late at all. In fact, she was early.

It felt funny to sit on the same old bus, wearing her same old school uniform, and carrying her same old backpack, knowing that inside the bag were her pink-and-green pajamas. What if she got to school and Mrs. Delano asked her to fetch something and she accidentally pulled out her new blue underwear instead?

She would die!

Or what if somebody found the box of chocolates for Ching Ching's mom and ate them, and she had nothing to give her? Or what if . . .

Olivia was not very good at relaxing.

By the time the bus arrived outside school, she was exhausted. She had thought up a hundred different disasters and had worried about each and every one, and it wasn't even eight o'clock yet.

Olivia dragged her bag off the bus. She was starting to feel slightly sick.

Maybe it wasn't such a good idea to sleep over at Ching Ching's, even though they were best friends. What if she and Ching Ching had a fight and they weren't even friends by the time her mom came to pick them up from school? Maybe she should tell Ching Ching that she had changed her mind. She could just give the chocolates to Ching Ching, and then phone her mom and say she would come home for dinner after all.

Across the playground, she saw Ching Ching waving at her, a huge smile on her face. Ching Ching's mom was a teacher and her dad was the principal, so Ching Ching and her brothers were always at school early.

"Hi, Olivia!" said Ching Ching, running over. "Isn't tonight going to be cool?"

"Yeah," said Olivia, running to meet her halfway. "It's going to be the best!"

She gave Ching Ching a hug and threw

her bag under a tree, and they went to play with the other kids until the bell rang.

The last day of school always dragged on forever. Everyone was itching to get out and be on vacation, but first they had to empty their lockers, tidy up the classroom, and collect all the art they had done that year.

Nobody could concentrate.

Dylan kept pestering Mrs. Delano, asking, "But why, miss? It's the last day of school. Can't we just play?"

By lunchtime, Mrs. Delano had given up.

"OK," she said. "You win. We've done enough and it's too hot to work anyway."

So they spent the rest of the day singing and talking about what everyone was doing for the holidays.

When it was time to leave, everyone was lined up and ready to go. Bags on their shoulders, they crowded at the school gates, straining their ears for the bell.

Come on, bell!
RING!

"There it is!" yelled someone, and they were off, flying out to freedom. Some ran to buses, and others went up the hill to the train station. Some walked home, and some, like Olivia and Ching Ching, waited to be picked up.

Ching Ching's parents both worked at the high school where Ching Ching's brothers went. Ching Ching was adopted and didn't look anything like her brothers. They were big, loud boys, all with the same short, spiky blond hair. Their names were Henry, Daniel, and William.

Olivia had met them lots of times before, of course. The first time had been at Ching Ching's birthday party at the zoo.

The boys were funny and rough, and had teased Ching Ching, picking her up and carrying her around the zoo, shouting to one another.

"Throw her to the seals!"

"No—too little! Not enough for a seal to eat. Here—catch!"

And Daniel had thrown—actually *thrown*—Ching Ching to Henry. Olivia had been astonished, watching her friend sail through the air like a doll. And Henry had caught her and called to William, "Should we chuck her to the monkeys?"

"Yeah!" said William. "She looks like a monkey."

"Smells like one, too," said Daniel.

"Let's go!" said Henry, and all three boys had carried Ching Ching away, hooting and chattering like monkeys as they went.

Olivia had been so upset, she was nearly in tears. How could they be so horrible to Ching Ching? And on her birthday!

But Ching Ching had come back giggling, sitting on William's shoulders, and waving to everyone.

So they weren't bad boys, exactly. It's just that Olivia didn't have any brothers and wasn't quite sure what to make of them.

CHAPTER THREE

"Hey!" said Ching Ching. "There they are!"

She pointed to a car slowly driving by, looking for somewhere to park. Olivia could see that it was full of Ching Ching's brothers. Ching Ching's mom waved her hand out the driver's window.

"Come on," said Ching Ching, and they ran to the car.

Mrs. Adams parked the car a long, long

way up the street from the school. Ching Ching and Olivia were puffing by the time they got there.

It was a hot summer afternoon, and their backpacks were heavy with all the things they had brought home from their desks and lockers. Olivia had her clothes for the sleepover, too, so her bag was bulging at its zipper.

Henry was sitting up front next to Mrs. Adams, and Daniel and William and their backpacks were filling the backseat, so Ching Ching and Olivia decided to sit in the special backwards-facing seats in the hatchback.

Olivia loved sitting back there, watching

the traffic come towards them, waving to the drivers in the cars behind as they waited at the lights. Mrs. Adams opened the back and helped them climb in.

"Hello, Olivia," she said, after kissing Ching Ching.

"Hello, Mrs. Adams," said Olivia.

"Now," said Mrs. Adams, "did you remember everything?"

Standing behind her, Ching Ching rolled her eyes at Olivia. Olivia tried not to laugh.

"Yes, I think so," said Olivia.

"Your pajamas?" said Mrs. Adams.

"Yes."

"Your toothbrush?"

"Ye—" Olivia began, but then stopped.

Her hand covered her mouth. Her eyes were as round as saucers. She felt herself blushing from her neck to her hair. She was horrified—she had forgotten her toothbrush.

"Oh, no," she said sadly.

"That's OK," said Mrs. Adams. "I have

to stop at some stores on the way home anyway. We'll buy you a toothbrush there."

"I'm so sorry," said Olivia.

"It's no problem," said Mrs. Adams. "You jump in with Ching Ching and we'll be off."

Olivia was miserable. She had messed up her sleepover with Ching Ching even before they got to her house. How could she be so forgetful? How could she have left her toothbrush behind? She had been so careful with everything else. She felt like crying.

"Don't worry," said Ching Ching. "I always forget my toothbrush. That's why my mom asked."

But it was so embarrassing and Olivia couldn't be cheered up. If only she knew that things were about to get worse!

CHAPTER FOUR

Mrs. Adams pulled into the parking lot, and all the kids streamed out. She sent Henry and William to the farmer's market to buy some potatoes, green beans, and broccoli. She sent Daniel to the supermarket for milk and rice, and she went with the girls to the pharmacy to pick up some pills for Mr. Adams and a toothbrush for Olivia. Ching Ching found a purple one with stars.

"You have to get this one, Mom," she said. "Please? I have a pink one like this and now Olivia and I can have the same."

So Mrs. Adams bought the toothbrush and they met the boys back at the butcher's. When the butcher saw them all standing there—Henry and William with the vegetables, Daniel with the milk and rice, and Mrs. Adams with the girls—he looked amazed and said, "What a lot of children!"

He leaned over the counter and smiled at Olivia.

"And you're having a friend over to play! Aren't you lucky!" he said.

Oh, this was bad! Too, too terrible.

Olivia looked at Mrs. Adams and her

long, blonde hair and light blue eyes. She looked at Henry, Daniel, and William. They had blond hair and light blue eyes, too.

She looked at Ching Ching with her shiny black hair and dark brown eyes and realized that to strangers, Ching Ching did not look like she belonged. Instead, the butcher thought Olivia was Mrs. Adams's daughter and Ching Ching was just a friend.

This was much, much worse than forgetting her toothbrush. Worse even than the thought of Henry, Daniel, and William accidentally seeing her underwear.

She looked sideways at Ching Ching to see if she was angry, or if she was as upset and embarrassed as Olivia was, but Ching

Ching was looking at her mom with an odd smile on her face.

Mrs. Adams looked at the butcher and said, "What?!"

Mrs. Adams hugged Ching Ching tightly to her.

"Only this one is mine," she said loudly. "I don't know where the rest of them came from."

Ching Ching giggled in her mom's arms.

"Really?" said the butcher, looking surprised.

"Yes, it's true," said Henry. "We're all adopted, except for Ching Ching."

"Oh," said the butcher. "Well. What can I get you?"

"Three pounds of sausage, please," said Mrs. Adams.

Back in the car, Olivia whispered to Ching Ching, "That was awful."

"Oh, we don't care," laughed Ching Ching. "It happens all the time. Mom made it into a game and now the boys compete to see who can say the silliest thing with a straight face. Henry always wins, of course."

CHAPTER FIVE

Ching Ching's house was very different from Olivia's. At home, it was just Olivia and her mom. They lived in a small apartment. They had one bedroom each, a living room where they had their dinner at the coffee table in front of the TV, and a balcony where they hung their laundry and grew herbs in pots. Everything was crowded, but very neat.

Ching Ching's house was much bigger. There were four bedrooms. One for Mr. and Mrs. Adams, one for Henry, one that Daniel and William shared, and one for Ching Ching.

They had a huge kitchen and living room, and a big backyard with trees and a swimming pool.

There was lots of space, but everything was untidy and cluttered. There were books and papers on every surface, footballs and tennis balls and sneakers all over the place, coffee mugs and pencil cases and calculators and toys, and even pieces of cold toast. It was a mess!

Olivia loved it. She was a quiet girl, but

secretly she loved all the noise and chaos of Ching Ching's house.

At her house, Olivia would have some fruit and yogurt for an afternoon snack, and then she would do her homework until her mom came home from work. Then they'd cook dinner together and watch TV.

At Ching Ching's house, Mrs. Adams gave them cookies and sponge cake for an

This is the life!

afternoon snack and sent them all outside. The boys played soccer and Olivia and Ching Ching swam in the pool until Mr. Adams came home from being principal.

Then they all sat down to dinner at the dining table. Olivia's mom cooked spicy things like chili beans and curry, and they served up dinner straight from the pots on the stove. If Olivia wanted seconds, she had to go back to the kitchen.

Mrs. Adams cooked very different food in enormous pots. The food was laid out on the table in serving dishes and everyone helped themselves. That night, they were having sausage, mashed potatoes, beans and broccoli.

The mashed potatoes were OK, and Olivia was used to beans and broccoli, but her mom never cooked sausage. Olivia really didn't like sausage, but Mrs. Adams put some on her plate without asking, and now she had to eat it.

She looked around the table. Mr. Adams and Henry were putting barbeque sauce on their sausage. Mrs. Adams was sprinkling hers with salt and pepper. Ching Ching was having ketchup.

"Do you want some?" she asked Olivia.

"Yes, please," said Olivia.

She liked ketchup, and maybe if she had enough of it, she could get through the sausage. She took the bottle from

Ching Ching. It was a big bottle, but it was nearly empty and the ketchup was taking forever to trickle out. Olivia shook it gently over her plate.

Nothing.

She shook it again.

"Where's the ketchup?" said Daniel.

"Olivia's using it," said Ching Ching.

"Hurry up," said Daniel, rolling his eyes.

Olivia blushed. She could feel everyone looking at her and the stupid bottle of ketchup. The ketchup still hadn't come out.

"Daniel," said Mr. Adams. "Don't be so rude. Take your time, Olivia. Daniel's in no hurry."

"Yes, I am," said Daniel. "I'm starving.

Look, just give the bottle a good thump," he said to Olivia.

Olivia wished she'd never come. Or that Daniel would be quiet. Or at the very least, that the ketchup would come out!

She hit the bottle hard, and then—SPLAT!

A huge dollop of ketchup spurted out of the bottle all over her plate, making a disgusting sound. It covered all three sausages, all the beans, and most of the mashed potatoes.

"Oh, come on!" said Daniel. "Have you left any for us?"

"Daniel!" said Mr. Adams. "Enough!"

Ching Ching poked her tongue out at

her brother. Olivia passed him the ketchup, not even looking at him.

"But, Dad," said Daniel, "you never let us have that much ketchup. You always say we can only have a dab."

Olivia just wanted to disappear.

Dinner was a disaster.

She tried to pretend that she liked having great pools of ketchup all over her food. She cut up the first sausage and ate a piece. It was dripping with ketchup. *It's not too bad*, she told herself.

The boys were talking to their dad, and Ching Ching was telling her mom about school, so no one was left to talk to Olivia. Good. She kept her head down and worked through the sausage, covering each bite in ketchup.

By the time she finished her dinner, she felt ill. She never wanted to taste ketchup again. Her throat was burning with it. More than anything in the world, Olivia wanted her mom to phone up and say she needed Olivia back home right away.

"Has everyone had enough to eat?" said Mrs. Adams.

"That was great," said Mr. Adams.

William groaned and patted his belly. Henry burped.

"Henry!" said Mrs. Adams. "Olivia, dear, would you like some more?"

Olivia shook her head firmly. *No way*, she thought.

"I mean, no thanks," she said, trying to sound polite.

"OK, then," said Mrs. Adams. "Clear the table."

The Adams had no television, but they did have a dishwasher. After dinner, each person rinsed their own plate and stacked it in the dishwasher.

When the table was cleared, Mrs. Adams brought a tub of ice cream and a package of waffle cones to the table.

"One ice cream cone each," she said. "And you can eat them outside."

She made up the cones and passed them one by one along the table.

"Now, shoo!" she said. "I need some peace and quiet."

CHAPTER SIX

Outside, it was still light. The sun was setting, though, and the sky was pink and orange over the trees.

Henry, Daniel, and William ate their ice cream as fast as they could and went back to playing soccer. Ching Ching and Olivia made their ice cream last as long as possible and then decided to go for another swim.

"It's so nice to swim as it gets dark," said Ching Ching. "The water's so warm, and you can just lie on your back and watch the birds go by and the stars come out."

Olivia agreed. They paddled and talked and looked at the sky and, except for the boys shouting as they played soccer, it was very peaceful.

After a while, it was too dark for the boys to see the ball and they packed up and went back inside. It was really quiet by the pool now, and a tiny bit spooky.

"Do you ever think," said Olivia, "you could just sink under the water and never come up?"

"Yeah," said Ching Ching. "You could

swim so deep you got sucked down that big drain."

They shuddered happily at the thought. They did this sometimes—talked about scary things to see how much they could frighten themselves.

"And the next day, there'd be nothing

but your pigtail stuck in the pool filter," said Olivia.

"And then one foot would be washed up on a beach, miles and miles away," said Ching Ching.

"Eeew!" they said together, laughing, but holding on tight to the edge of the pool, just in case.

"We should sleep out here tonight," said Ching Ching.

"Yeah?" said Olivia. "What about mosquitoes?"

"We would sleep right under the sheets," said Ching Ching. "Maybe we could burn one of those smelly candles, too."

"And we could stay up all night and watch the sun rise," said Olivia.

"Ching Ching!"

It was Mrs. Adams calling from the backdoor.

"Time for bed. You and Olivia, out of the pool, now!"

"You can *so* tell your mom is a teacher," said Olivia.

They got out of the pool and found that their fingers and toes had gotten wrinkly. The air was cool on their wet skin and by the time they got inside, they were shivering.

They stood together in front of the bathroom mirror with their matching toothbrushes, giggling and trying to brush their chattering teeth. They brushed their hair and Ching Ching tied hers back in long, low braids for bed. They changed into their pajamas and decided it was too much effort to sleep outside that night.

Ching Ching had bunk beds, and because it was the first time Olivia had slept over, she got to sleep on top.

"I always read for a while before I go to sleep," said Ching Ching. "Would you like to borrow a book, or do you have one?"

"Borrow one, please," said Olivia, because Ching Ching always had lots of books. Olivia supposed it was because both her parents worked at the school.

Olivia found one about a girl who ran

away to sea on a pirate ship. It looked very interesting, but when she climbed up the ladder to her bed and got in under the covers, she didn't feel like reading.

At home, in her own bed, her mom usually came in and kissed her good night. Sometimes they talked about their day, sometimes Olivia read out loud from a book, and sometimes her mom told her a story instead. She remembered how her mom had said that morning that she would miss Olivia.

Olivia realized this was the first time in her life she had gone to bed without even a hug from her mom. She felt a bit sad and lonely.

Outside in the pool, talking with Ching Ching, Olivia had forgotten all about the embarrassment of dinner. Now, lying in bed, she started thinking about it all over again. She felt her stomach shrink into a cold, hard ball.

It was too late to call her mom and ask to go home. She was stuck here. Daniel was horrible, Mrs. Adams probably thought she

was silly for forgetting her toothbrush, and everyone thought she was greedy for eating all that ketchup.

How could she sleep with all these thoughts in her head? She wanted to cry, but she didn't want Ching Ching to hear her. In the bunk below, Ching Ching switched off her lamp.

"Good night, Olivia," she said.

"Good night," said Olivia, hoping her voice sounded normal.

Olivia turned off her lamp, too. The room was very dark now. How long until morning? Olivia rolled on to her side and pretended she was in her own bed. She imagined her own room, her own toys, her own blankets over her. She imagined her mom in the room next door, and it must have worked because very soon she was fast asleep.

CHAPTER
SEVEN

Olivia had strange dreams. She woke up suddenly, and for a moment she couldn't figure out where she was. The bed was on the wrong side of the room, and up too high, and her pillow smelled funny. It was still dark. She could hear a clock ticking and someone below her breathing.

Oh, yes—she was at Ching Ching's house. She couldn't remember her dream

but she felt wide awake. What time was it? Definitely too early to get up.

At home, she would have gone to the bathroom and then maybe crept into her mom's bed for a cuddle until morning.

That wasn't a good thing to think about right now. It just made her feel sorry for herself. Instead, she would think of warm, sleepy things. Hot chocolate before bedtime, sheepskin slippers, the sound of heavy rain on the roof . . .

When Olivia opened her eyes again, it was now Saturday morning. The sunlight was bright through Ching Ching's curtains and the blankets felt too warm.

Olivia listened. The house was still very quiet. Not sleeping quiet, but empty quiet.

She peered over the edge of her bunk bed and looked for Ching Ching. Her bed was a tumble of blankets and sheets, but there was no Ching Ching in it.

Olivia couldn't decide whether to get

up or stay where she was and wait for Ching Ching to come back. Would it be worse to lie in bed for ages and have Ching Ching waiting for her, or worse to go down the hallway and bump into Henry or Daniel or William while she was wearing her pink-and-green pajamas?

She was sitting up in bed, the top of her head almost brushing the ceiling, when Ching Ching appeared at the doorway.

"Oh, you're up," she said. "Good. We have the house to ourselves."

"Where's everyone gone?" asked Olivia.

"The boys play sports on Saturday, so Dad has taken Henry to one field, and Mom has taken Daniel and William to another. They'll be back for lunch, though."

Phew! Olivia could avoid horrible Daniel at least until lunchtime. She climbed down from the bed.

"The boys have eaten all the good cereal," said Ching Ching. "There's only bread left for us."

"Are you allowed to use the stove?" asked Olivia.

"Probably," said Ching Ching. "Why?"

"I could make us French toast. Mom and I make it all the time."

"Cool," said Ching Ching. "That's way better than cereal. What do you need?"

"Eggs, milk, and butter," said Olivia.

"And a frying pan. And bread, of course."

Olivia started mixing the eggs and milk, and soaking the bread.

"While I'm making this," she said, "you should find some cinnamon to go with it."

Ching Ching looked around.

"We don't have any," she said.

"Maple syrup?"

"Nope," said Ching Ching. "What about honey?"

"That will work," said Olivia, dropping the first slice of bread into the frying pan. It sizzled nicely.

"We've got bananas and strawberries, too," said Ching Ching.

"Perfect," said Olivia, turning the toast.

In the end, it was a beautiful breakfast.
Olivia cooked two slices of French toast for
each of them, and Ching Ching decorated
them with honey and slices of fruit.

"Wait," said Ching Ching. "One more
thing."

She pulled a can of whipped cream out

of the fridge and squirted a long squiggle onto each plate.

"That," said Olivia, "is so fancy."

"Yeah," said Ching Ching.

"Almost too fancy to eat."

"Yeah," said Ching Ching.

They were quiet for a second, admiring their work. Then Ching Ching caught Olivia's eye and smiled.

"No," she said. "I can eat it."

"Me, too," said Olivia.

They sat by the pool, dangling their legs in the water and eating the toast off plates balanced on their laps.

"This is so nice," said Olivia.

"Yeah," said Ching Ching. "I wish we could do this every Saturday. No boys yelling, no parents nagging."

"Is it nice having a big family?" asked Olivia.

"Mostly. I get tired of being the smallest sometimes, though."

Olivia was the biggest and the smallest rolled into one in her family, but she thought she understood what Ching Ching meant.

"Still," she said. "I bet you don't get bored."

"No," said Ching Ching, eating the last strawberry on her plate.

There was a loud bang from the house

as the front door slammed shut. Then Mrs. Adams yelled out from the backdoor, "Ching Ching!"

"Oh, no," said Ching Ching. "They're back already and we haven't even had our Saturday morning swim yet."

CHAPTER EIGHT

"Ching Ching," said Mrs. Adams, when they were back inside the house. "Have you been using the stove?"

Olivia froze.

In Mrs. Adams's hands were the dirty plates from breakfast, and in the kitchen, sitting in the sink, was the dirty frying pan she had used to cook the French toast.

"No," said Ching Ching.

Olivia couldn't believe her ears. Mrs. Adams looked angry. No, more than angry. She looked wild and fierce.

"Ching Ching," said Mrs. Adams. "Don't lie to me. Have you been using the stove?"

"I promise," said Ching Ching. "I never touched the stove. Did I, Olivia?"

Mrs. Adams turned to Olivia, and Olivia was so frightened, she could hardly breathe.

"Is Ching Ching telling the truth?" asked Mrs. Adams.

"Yes," said Olivia in a shaky voice.

"See?" said Ching Ching to her mom.

"Well, then," said Mrs. Adams. "Who made all this mess?"

"I don't know," said Ching Ching.

She was about to say more, but Olivia spoke up.

"*I* did," Olivia said.

She didn't know what would happen to her now, but she couldn't keep quiet. She would rather die than have Mrs. Adams angry with her, but she never lied to her mom

and didn't know how *not* to tell the truth.

"I used the stove," she said quietly.

Mrs. Adams looked at her. Ching Ching stared at her.

"*You*, Olivia?" said Mrs. Adams.

"I cooked French toast," said Olivia.

She looked at Ching Ching, but her friend's face was a careful blank.

"I see," said Mrs. Adams. "Didn't Ching Ching tell you she isn't allowed to use the stove without a grown-up in the house?"

Olivia shook her head.

"I mean," she said quickly, not wanting to get Ching Ching in trouble, "she thought perhaps it might be all right."

Mrs. Adams sighed and looked at the

two of them.

"I'm sorry to say this, Olivia," she said. "But Ching Ching did not tell you the truth. In this house, children are not allowed to cook on their own."

"I'm sorry," said Olivia, almost in a whisper.

"Ching Ching," said Mrs. Adams, "I'm so angry with you right now. Did you know the stove was left on? When I came in, the burner was glowing red. That's how fires start and houses burn down, and people get very badly hurt."

Ching Ching said nothing.

"Well, what do you have to say for yourself?" asked Mrs. Adams.

"The boys ate all the good cereal," said Ching Ching. "There was nothing else for us to eat."

"That's not quite true, is it?" said Mrs. Adams. "You could have used the toaster. Or the microwave. You could have had banana sandwiches. You could have had milkshakes. You weren't going to starve."

Mrs. Adams opened the fridge to show Ching Ching all the things she could have had for breakfast.

"Look," she said. "Orange juice, watermelon, cheese, tomatoes. You could have had—hey! Did you eat all the strawberries?"

Oh, no, thought Olivia.

"That's it," said Mrs. Adams, slamming the fridge. "Go to your room now, Ching Ching! I'm just furious."

The two girls fled.

CHAPTER NINE

In Ching Ching's room, Olivia finally started to breathe again.

"I thought your mom was going to kill us," she said.

"She would have if you'd kept talking," said Ching Ching.

"Me?" said Olivia. "What did I do?"

"Only told her everything," said Ching Ching. "If you'd kept quiet, we'd be outside right now, swimming."

Olivia was shocked.

"What are you talking about?" she said. "I left the stove on and we weren't even supposed to touch it!"

"So?" said Ching Ching.

"And you lied to your mom!"

"Sort of," said Ching Ching. "But it wasn't a big lie."

Olivia stared at her friend. She thought Ching Ching was crazy to lie to Mrs. Adams.

Ching Ching sighed.

"Look," she said. "You don't have any brothers or sisters, so you probably don't understand. When you have a big family, you don't need to get into trouble. Mom

and Dad are so busy, and there are so many of us, you can just do what you want. As long as everyone keeps quiet, Mom and Dad can never figure out who did what and so no one gets the blame."

"That's terrible," said Olivia, but she could also see that it was a bit exciting, too.

"But you told on us, so now we have to sit here," said Ching Ching.

"Your mom would have known it was us, though," said Olivia. "We were the only ones home."

"Probably," said Ching Ching. "But then maybe she left with Daniel and William before Dad and Henry left, so maybe it wasn't us after all."

Olivia thought about her place, with just her and her mom. Her mom could tell exactly what Olivia did—every dropped sock, every wet towel, every crumb on the coffee table. Who else could it be?

It was hard to imagine what it would

be like to live in Ching Ching's house. You could get away with so many things!

On the other hand, maybe that made it lonely sometimes. Olivia liked the idea that her mom knew everything about her.

"Anyway," said Ching Ching. "It was worth it. That was the best breakfast I've ever had."

"I can't believe you," said Olivia.

"I know," said Ching Ching. "I'm really, really naughty. But guess what? I'm also full of French toast and strawberries, and I don't care."

Olivia laughed. She couldn't help it. Ching Ching really was terrible, but she was so funny, too. Olivia knew they were stuck in Ching Ching's room because they were in trouble, but right now, giggling with her best friend, even that seemed kind of fun.

CHAPTER TEN

They stayed in Ching Ching's room for ages, reading books and playing with Ching Ching's toys. They heard Mr. Adams come home with Henry, and then all three brothers and Mr. Adams went outside for a swim. Ching Ching and Olivia watched them from the bedroom window.

The boys were diving and doing cannonballs into the pool and water was splashing up in waves all over the sides. Mr. Adams was sitting on the steps in the shallow end, the water up to his chest, cheering the boys on.

"Well done, William!" he called. "That was the biggest splash yet. Watch out, Henry! Daniel's in your way."

"I'm bored now," said Ching Ching. "Don't you think we've been stuck in here long enough?"

"Maybe," said Olivia doubtfully.

In fact, she felt safe in Ching Ching's room. Outside, Mrs. Adams was mad at them, and Daniel might embarrass her again. Who knew what other trouble was waiting?

In here, she had Ching Ching all to herself, and they could play until her mom came to take her home.

"We could do another magazine quiz," she said, but Ching Ching was already opening the bedroom door.

The smell of frying onions drifted in and Ching Ching stood with her head in the hallway, sniffing deeply.

"Oh," she said with longing. "Hamburgers. My favorite."

It seemed like a long time since breakfast, and Olivia's stomach growled.

"I'd love a hamburger," she said. "But my mom's coming to pick me up soon."

"Before lunch or after?" asked Ching

Ching.

"I'm not sure."

"But you will stay for hamburgers, won't you?"

"I hope so," said Olivia, because the smell was getting stronger and more delicious every minute.

"Oops," said Ching Ching, jumping back inside the room and shutting the door. "Mom's coming."

They scurried onto Ching Ching's bed and pretended to be reading books just as Mrs. Adams opened the door.

"OK, you two," she said. "Lunchtime. Olivia, do you know what time your mom is coming to pick you up?"

"No," said Olivia.

"Well, you've got time for a burger, anyway. Your mom can join us if she gets here early. And then," she said more sternly, looking at Ching Ching and the mess in her bedroom, "you can come back here and tidy up a bit."

Lunch was actually fun. They put their hamburgers together on the kitchen table. Olivia tried to make sure Daniel was nowhere near when she got her burger, and she avoided the ketchup, too!

She was just putting some lettuce on her bun and trying to decide whether to have pickles and cheese when someone beside her said, "Do you want some lemonade?"

Olivia looked up and froze. It was Daniel, pouring lemonade into plastic cups. Was he teasing her? Was he being rude somehow? What should she say? Daniel just smiled and passed her a cup.

"Thanks," said Olivia. She didn't know

what else to say.

She suddenly thought that maybe it didn't really matter about the ketchup after all.

She went out with her burger and found Ching Ching sitting under a tree, already eating.

Olivia realized her sleepover was almost over. Part of her felt glad. It would be nice to be back home where she knew all the rules and liked all the food.

Another part of her, though, felt sad because she would miss Ching Ching. She would even miss the things that frightened her—Mrs. Adams when she's angry, Daniel, and the brave and lonely feelings she had sleeping in Ching Ching's top bunk.

Mr. Adams called out from the back door. "Olivia! Look who's here!"

Olivia looked up, and there was her mom. She looked very short next to Mr. Adams, and Olivia had forgotten how pretty she was.

"Oh, no!" said Ching Ching. "Now you'll have to go home, I guess."

"Yeah," said Olivia, and she couldn't tell if she was happy or sad.

They wandered back towards the house.

"Hi, Mom," said Olivia.

"Hi, baby," said her mom.

Olivia didn't want to hug her in front of everybody. Luckily, her mom seemed to know this.

"Did you have a good time?" asked her mom.

"Yeah," said Olivia.

"Did you behave yourself?"

"Um, yeah," said Olivia, looking sideways at Mrs. Adams.

Mrs. Adams laughed.

"She's been a peach," she said. "They've been up to a few tricks, but nothing too terrible."

Olivia smiled with relief.

"Have you packed?" said her mom.

"Not yet."

"Go on, then. I'll stay and chat with Mrs. Adams while you do."

Thanks for having me.

In Ching Ching's room, Olivia found the box of chocolates as she packed her pajamas.

"Oh, I forgot to give these to your mom," she said.

"Let's keep them," said Ching Ching. "Or we could tell Mom she can only have them if she promises you can sleep over next weekend."

"Or you could sleep over at my house," said Olivia. "I could make French toast again for breakfast."

Ching Ching dragged Olivia's bag to the front door. For some reason, it didn't seem to zip up as well as it had the day before. Olivia's pink-and-green pajamas stuck out the top, but now she didn't care who saw them.

"Thank you for having me," she said to Mrs. Adams, giving her the chocolates.

"Oh, lovely," said Mrs. Adams. "These will be even better than strawberries after dinner tonight."

Olivia blushed. She took her bag from Ching Ching and followed her mom out the front door.

"Bye," she said, waving.

She felt happy and brave and somehow more grown-up than yesterday.

"I'm glad you had fun," said her mom as they got into the car.

"Yes," said Olivia. "I really did."

THE END

BY
THALIA KALKIPSAKIS

ILLUSTRATED BY
ASH OSWALD

SQUARE
FISH

FEIWEL AND FRIENDS
NEW YORK

SQUARE
FISH

An Imprint of Macmillan
175 Fifth Avenue
New York, NY 10010
mackids.com

Library of Congress Cataloging-in-Publication Data Available

ISBN 978-1-250-11262-0

First published in Australia by E2, an imprint of Hardie Grant
Egmont. Illustration and design by Ash Oswald.

First published in the United States by Feiwel and Friends
First Square Fish Edition: 2013
Square Fish Reissue Edition: 2016
Square Fish logo designed by Filomena Tuosto

1   3   5   7   9   10   8   6   4   2

AR: 3.2 / F&P: L

CHAPTER ONE

My big sister Hannah hates me and I know why. It's because I was born after her.

When Hannah was three, I was born. Everyone said I was *sooooooo cute!* Mom says they stopped saying Hannah was cute, so she threw all my baby clothes down the toilet.

I look younger than I really am. I'm nine years old, but sometimes people think

I look six or seven.

Hannah calls me a baby doll, but she doesn't mean it in a nice way. She says I should try to look my age, but it's not my fault! I can't change how I look.

But now, it's even worse than ever. Hannah cut off my hair and Mom went crazy on her. Then Hannah stopped talking to me.

Strange, isn't it? Hannah cut off my hair and got into trouble, and she blames me for it!

She must really hate me, that girl. Let me explain.

We were watching TV and a show came on about hair. It said that a haircut can change the way you look. It can make you look older or younger.

Hannah said, "Maybe if we cut your hair, people wouldn't think you're so cute anymore!"

"Yeah," I said, not really listening.

Hannah turned off the TV. "Aren't you sick of people saying how cute you look?" she asked.

"Yeah," I said again, but now I *was* listening.

"So why don't we cut your hair short, so you look your age?" Hannah said.

I wasn't sure. It sounded exciting, cutting my hair. I liked the idea of doing something different and looking older. But it's a big

thing to cut off all your hair. And I've had
long hair all my life.

"But what would Mom say?" I said.

"Mom!" Hannah rolled her eyes. Her
hair is dark and shoulder length. It kinks
up around her ears.

"Why do you always worry what Mom

thinks? It's not Mom's hair, " she said.

She had a point. It wasn't Mom's hair, it was *my* hair.

"Come on, let's do it." Hannah's eyes looked bright with excitement.

It was exciting to do something like this together, just her and me. It felt a bit like the stories you read of sisters going shopping and trying on clothes together. It felt good—like Hannah liked me.

It also seemed a little naughty to do something without Mom knowing.

"OK," I said. "Let's do it."

Hannah smiled.

I bet my eyes looked as bright and excited as Hannah's.

CHAPTER TWO

I'll always remember the sound of the scissors cutting through my hair.

It was a kind of a crunching sound. You'd probably expect a *snip snip* kind of sound. But there was so much hair bunched together that the scissors made a sliding, crunching sound as Hannah cut.

My hair was tied in two pigtails. Hannah said she would cut off each pigtail, and then clean up my hair after that.

When she had cut off the first pigtail, Hannah held up the hair for me to see.

"Say good-bye to your hair, Cassie," she said.

I was giggling and waving good-bye when Mom walked in.

All of a sudden, everything changed.

Mom looked at the bunch of my hair in Hannah's hand.

"Hannah!" she said. "What are you doing?"

"Calm down, Mom." It sounded like Hannah knew Mom would yell. "Cassie's not a little girl anymore."

"What!" I could hear Mom breathing

heavily as she pulled at the hair behind my ear. "Apart from doing this without asking, haven't you two heard of hairdressers?"

Hannah shrugged. I didn't say anything. I was surprised Mom was so angry.

Mom was still fussing behind my ear.

"I'm going to clean it up," Hannah said, but her voice sounded unsure now.

"Look how short it is here!" Mom yelled in my ear. "How on earth are you going to clean up this piece?"

Hannah leaned in and started breathing heavily into my ear, too.

Then she said, "How did that piece get so short?"

Now I was worried.

"When you cut hair in a pigtail," Mom said quietly, "you end up with different lengths. All the hair is pulled from different parts of the head, so you end up with some long pieces and some REALLY SHORT PIECES!"

Hannah gasped.

I jumped up and started yelling, too.

"Hannah, what did you do?" I yelled. I suddenly felt scared and angry.

"It's OK," Hannah said, but her voice sounded wobbly. "I can fix it."

As my mind raced, I felt the short hair behind my ear. In some places, it was so short it felt prickly. Why had Hannah cut it like that?

Then I realized what Hannah had done.

"You tricked me!" I yelled. "You did this to me because you hate me looking cute!"

Hannah rolled her eyes. "Yes, I hate you looking cute," she yelled back. "You're nine years old!"

"You did this to me on purpose!"

Now I was crying. Half of my hair was gone, and my big sister had done it to me because she hates me.

"You want me to look ugly!"

"Yeah, right," Hannah yelled. "I'm the EVIL BIG SISTER." She was yelling even louder than Mom or me.

Then Hannah ran to her room and slammed the door.

Mom looked at me and shook her head.

"I'll call the hairdresser," she said.

When we came home from the hairdresser, Hannah was still in her bedroom. My room is next to Hannah's, but I couldn't hear any noise coming from next door.

I looked in the mirror. A stranger with short hair stared back at me. My hair was so short, it looked like it had been shaved in some places. I looked like a different person.

What would Dad think?

He calls me his beautiful little girl, but I didn't feel beautiful or little anymore.

We were going to see Dad and his girlfriend Felicity over the weekend. I wondered how much my hair would grow in three days.

I still felt angry that Hannah had tricked me. She had planned it all along. She was so mean!

I lay down on my bed, feeling bad. My long hair was gone and Hannah hated me more than ever.

❁

CHAPTER THREE

For dinner, we had my favorite food —pizza.

Mom kept saying, "Cheer up, Cassie. You look great!" But she looked tired and sad.

Hannah just stared at her plate. She loves pizza, too, but she only ate one slice. Then she went back to her bedroom.

After dinner, I turned on the TV. I sat in the best chair, even though it was Hannah's turn. I wanted Hannah to walk in and tell me it was her turn in the chair. Then I would yell back at her, and ask her why she had cut my hair so short.

But Hannah didn't come in, so I turned off the TV.

I went to bed and tried to sleep.

I wanted the day to be over. But it was too early to sleep. I lay in the dark, feeling more and more angry.

Then I noticed something.

A tiny crack of light was coming from my closet.

My closet was built into the wall, so it was strange to see light coming from it. Where was the light coming from?

A toy? A flashlight? Maybe it was a magic door.

It was pretty dark in my room, but I could see OK. I crept along the carpet to where my closet meets the wall. Then I slid the door open, and waited.

Nothing happened.

The crack of light was coming from the side of the closet, right in front of me. I leaned in closer, trying to see better. The light seemed to get brighter.

What could the light be?

Suddenly, I understood. It made sense.

The light wasn't coming from inside my closet—it was coming from Hannah's room.

Hannah and I both have closets built into the same wall. Hannah's closet faces into her room and mine faces into my room.

I peered further into my closet. There was a gap between the edge of the closet and the wall. I could just see the gap on Hannah's side, too.

The light was coming from Hannah's room and through her closet. I could see her room through the gaps.

How strange! The builder must have made a mistake and not bothered to fix it.

Then I had an idea.

The gap wasn't very wide, but neither am I. I leaned forward until my head slipped through the gap. Then I turned my shoulders to the side and carefully slid my whole body through.

I was standing between the two closets in the wall. It felt a bit cramped and dusty. I barely had room to move. But it was exciting, like a tiny, secret room.

I squeezed my head through the gap leading to Hannah's closet and peeked out through the hanging clothes.

I felt like a secret spy.

I hadn't found a magic door but I had found something better—a secret door into Hannah's room!

Hannah was sitting on her bed and reading. I could just see part of Hannah's head, but I couldn't see what she was reading.

Hannah just sat there, turning the pages and reading. Nothing was happening, but I didn't feel bored. I felt good, like I had something really secret and useful.

Hannah didn't want to watch TV with

me. She didn't even want to talk to me.
But I could still watch her.

Then Hannah did something.

She picked her nose!

Then she wiped it on her bed. Yuck!

I stayed in the secret spot for a long
time, just watching.

CHAPTER FOUR

The next morning, I was extra slow walking to school. Hannah is supposed to walk with me before she heads off to high school. But today, she walked ahead without even looking at me.

I kicked at stones and shuffled my feet. I thought about telling Mom that Hannah hadn't walked with me to school.

I wanted Hannah to get into trouble

for being so mean. But I knew she would hate me even more if I told Mom.

When I finally made it to school, the bell had just rung.

Perfect timing.

I slipped into the end of the line, hoping no one would notice my hair.

My plan worked for about twenty seconds. That's how long it took to walk into the classroom and sit down.

Bec, who sits next to me, noticed right away.

"Cassie! Oh, look at your hair!" she said sadly. "It's all gone . . . your beautiful hair. . . ."

I didn't know what to say. I just wanted

Bec to stop talking about it. But by now, the whole class was staring at me.

Everyone was looking at me and talking about my hair.

"You cut your hair, Cassie!"

"Look at Cassie!"

I could feel my face turning red.

This is all Hannah's fault.

This was all Hannah's fault.

"Looks like you had a fight with a lawn mower," Adrian said. I don't like Adrian. He has dirty fingernails.

After that, nothing bad really happened. Mrs. Bonacci chose me to be snack monitor.

That was good.

At lunchtime, the girls were all really nice, too. They all said my hair looked good. They tried to make me feel better. Everyone kept touching it and saying how soft it felt.

At the end of the day, even Sam talked to me.

"See you tomorrow, funky girl," he said and smiled.

Wow, Sam noticed me.

I kind of like Sam, but that's a secret.

After school, walking with Mom through the grocery store was different, too. When I had long hair, old ladies would smile at me. Some would even try to talk to me. But none of them did that today. It was like they didn't notice me anymore.

The lady with lots of makeup who works at the deli always used to give me a piece of chicken to eat.

But not today. She didn't even recognize me!

The TV show was right—I really do look different with short hair. But more than that, people think I'm a different sort of person. They don't treat me like a little girl anymore.

I started to feel glad that people weren't treating me like a doll anymore. I didn't have to be the good little girl —I could just be myself.

Now I could start to grow up.

CHAPTER FIVE

When we got home from shopping, I was still feeling bad about Hannah. She was at band practice, so while Mom was putting the groceries away, I sneaked into Hannah's room. I wanted to see what she had been reading last night.

Hannah's room is always really messy. She has clothes all over the floor, and books and magazines all over her desk.

But she has some good pictures on her wall. There's even a picture of Orlando Towner. Hannah says he's the most gorgeous guy in the world, but I'm not sure what's so good about him.

There was only a clock radio on Hannah's bedside table. I searched around her desk and bookshelf. But none of the books there looked like the one that Hannah had been reading last night.

Then I looked under Hannah's bed.

There it was—the book from last night. Hannah had slipped it under her bed as though she didn't want Mom to know what she was reading.

I pulled the book out.

The cover said *Ghosts and Spirits—Real-Life Sightings.* There was a picture of an old-fashioned room with big windows and a fuzzy white splotch in the middle. I stared at the splotch, but it didn't look like a ghost to me.

I flicked through the book. It showed lots of splotches. I read about someone who used to hear ghosts walking down the hall.

Suddenly, I heard something.

I held my breath and listened.

There it was again. Voices.

Ghost voices?

No. Hannah must have come home and was talking to Mom in the kitchen.

I slipped the ghost book back under Hannah's bed and tiptoed to her door.

I was just about to sneak out when I heard the hall door open.

Oh, no! Hannah would see me if I opened her door now.

I was trapped in her room!

I stumbled back from Hannah's bedroom door, almost tripping on a pair of jeans. She was about to catch me sneaking around in her room.

Then I remembered my secret place.

There was a gap in the side of Hannah's closet, too. That's how I could see into her room last night.

I could hear Hannah walking down the hall. Quickly, I squeezed into Hannah's closet. I stepped on something that snapped under one foot, and crushed a box under the other, but I had no time to be careful.

I slipped into the secret space in the wall just as Hannah opened her door.

Phew...
just in time.

I held my breath and froze. If I could see through the gap, then Hannah could, too—if she looked carefully.

I pressed my back into the wall, trying to be as small and quiet as possible.

I couldn't see Hannah now, but I could hear some clothes rustling as though she was taking off her school uniform.

Would she come and look in the closet to choose some clothes?

I saw a flicker of dark hair as Hannah leaned down to pick up some jeans from the floor. I was lucky she was so messy.

I breathed as quietly as I could.

Hannah pulled something out of her bag. I realized she had no idea that I was there, hiding. Watching her.

This was amazing. I had already found out about the ghost book. What else could I learn about Hannah?

I felt as though the ghost book was important, but I couldn't think why.

I needed to watch Hannah some more.

CHAPTER SIX

At dinner, I told Mom about being snack monitor. I felt happy, and Mom seemed happy, too. Hannah just looked down at her fried rice without smiling.

"How was band practice?" I asked Hannah.

She glanced over at me. For a moment, I thought she wasn't going to answer at all. Then she looked back down at her rice.

"Fine," she said.

Mom sighed. She started looking sad again. I felt angry that Hannah could make us all feel bad.

"Pass the soy sauce, please," I said. I didn't really want any soy sauce, but it was right in front of Hannah. I wanted to see what she would do.

Hannah just kept eating.

Rude, huh?

Being ignored by Hannah was almost worse than when she cut my hair.

Mom shook her head and reached over to give me the soy sauce.

"Hannah's been chosen for the band concert," Mom said. "She's done really well."

Hannah would be really pleased with

that. She loves playing the flute. But she kept on staring at her rice and eating.

Mom sighed again.

Normally, I would have been happy for Hannah. But now things were different. I wasn't cute anymore, and I didn't want to be nice.

So I just shrugged and stared down at my rice like Hannah.

I couldn't see poor Mom because I was staring at my rice, but I could tell she wasn't smiling.

After dinner, Hannah went straight to her room. I was about to do the same when the phone rang.

It was Dad. He talked happily about our visit over the weekend. He was planning on taking us for a dim sum lunch, then to the park.

Dad asked how I was doing.

"Good," I said. "I was snack monitor today."

But I couldn't tell him about my hair.

What will
Dad say about
my hair?

Over the phone, Dad still thought I was
his beautiful little girl. In some ways, that
was nice.

"And I have a surprise, too," I said.

"Surprise, huh?" Dad said. "Sounds
interesting."

I could still be Dad's little girl for a few
more days. *Then* he would see the surprise.

While Hannah was talking to Dad,
I went to my room. It was dark now, but

I didn't turn the light on. Feeling like a spy, I slipped into my secret spot. Ready.

When Hannah went back to her room, she lay on her tummy on the bed and pulled out the ghost book. She loves that book.

I watched Hannah's legs on the bed and wondered why she read that book so much. Did she really think those white splotches in the pictures were ghosts?

Did Hannah believe ghosts were real?

As I watched Hannah from my secret spot, an idea came to me. I smiled to myself. It was the perfect way to find out if Hannah believed in ghosts. I waited for a while, watching Hannah. Then I did it.

Scratch, scratch, scratch.

I felt a bit silly, scratching the wall, but it was part of my new plan. Maybe Hannah would think I was a ghost in the wall. I wanted to see what she would do.

Scratch, scratch, scratch.

I waited. But Hannah kept reading. This was boring.

I tried one more time.

Scratch, scratch, scratch.

Suddenly, Hannah moved. She sat up on the bed, facing the closet.

I held my breath and did it one last time.

Scratch, scratch, scratch.

But Hannah just shrugged. She rolled over and kept on reading.

Maybe Hannah didn't believe in ghosts after all.

CHAPTER *SEVEN*

The next morning at breakfast, Hannah said, "I think there's a mouse in my closet."

I hid a smile.

"What!" said Mom. Mom's a neat freak, and really doesn't like mice. "Is there some food hidden under all that mess?" she asked Hannah.

"I don't think so." Hannah frowned down at her cornflakes.

"Well, let's have a cleanup," Mom said and rubbed her hands together. She liked the idea of cleaning Hannah's room.

"I'll do it tonight," Hannah said quickly. "OK? Don't go in my room."

Mom looked disappointed. "OK," she said sadly.

After school, Hannah started cleaning up her room. I didn't have to hide in the secret spot to know what Hannah was doing. I could hear her throwing things in the closet. Clean room, messy closet—that was Hannah.

While Hannah was cleaning, I went through my box of hair ties and clips. I put all the hair ties in a bag and put them in a drawer. It would be a long time before I could use them again.

My hair was almost too short even for the clips. I tried putting two in my hair. Maybe I could wear them tomorrow to see Dad. But they looked a bit silly. They suited a little girl with long hair.

After a while, I put all the clips away with the hair ties.

Then I looked around my room. It was totally different from Hannah's. There was a pile of teddy bears and dolls in one corner. Another corner had an old wooden stove that I used to play with. There was even a Bananas in Pajamas growth chart on the wall.

It looked like a baby's room.

I pulled down the Bananas in Pajamas chart and stared at the blank space on the wall. What should I put there instead? I didn't like Orlando Towner.

Who did I like?

After a while, I listened for Hannah.

I couldn't hear her throwing things in the closet anymore. Everything was quiet.

I turned out the light in my room and slid quietly into the secret spot. It was extra dark because Hannah's closet door was shut properly.

As my eyes got used to the darkness, I could see all the clothes and junk Hannah had thrown in the closet. There was even a bag and some clothes blocking the gap leading to Hannah's closet.

I smiled in the darkness. Hannah had cleaned up her room because of my scratching. That felt good—she couldn't ignore me completely.

What could I do next?

CHAPTER EIGHT

I stood in the darkness in my secret spot, thinking about ghosts again. If mice scratch, what noise do ghosts make?

They stomp around at night.

I couldn't see into Hannah's room, but that was OK. If her closet door was shut, then I was completely hidden, too.

I reached into her closet and thumped on the door.

Thump, thump, thump, thump.

Ha! Mice didn't thump. I waited, but nothing happened. Maybe Hannah wasn't in her room.

I tried again.

Thump, thump, thump, thump.

Still nothing.

Suddenly, Hannah's closet door slid open. A shoe and a CD stand toppled out onto Hannah's feet.

I blinked in the sudden light and leaned back into the shadows. Had Hannah seen me? I pushed my back into the wall behind me.

Everything was quiet.

I saw Hannah lift her arm to scratch her head. Then she leaned down to pick up the shoe and CD stand. She jammed them back into the closet and lay back down on the bed.

That had been close, but the hiding place had worked. Hannah hadn't seen me. She would never notice the gap if

I kept the light out in my room.

I leaned forward and peeked into Hannah's room. I could see her legs on the bed. She was on her tummy, facing the other way.

Hannah had left her closet door open, so now I couldn't reach it. It was open too far.

Instead, I reached down to touch the CD stand. It was lying down, folded shut. That was good. I didn't want the noise to come right from my hiding spot.

I couldn't lift the CD stand, but I gave it a wiggle and a shove. It rattled against the wooden floor.

Rattle, rattle, clang.

Right away, Hannah jumped back up. I couldn't see her, but I could hear her breathing now.

She stood in front of the closet for a while, and then she started pulling all her stuff out. Everything that had gone in came out again, plus all the things that were in there to start with.

She wasn't quiet about it, either. As Hannah pulled and rattled and threw, I slipped quietly out of the hiding space, back into my room.

Easy.

It seemed very tidy and peaceful in my room.

I switched on my reading lamp and

pretended to read as I listened to Hannah empty her closet.

She was making a lot of noise. Mom must have heard it, too.

"Hannah!" Mom didn't sound pleased. "What are you doing?"

I couldn't hear Hannah reply.

"You're supposed to be cleaning up this mess."

"Mom," Hannah was speaking softly. "There's something. . . ."

"What? A mouse?" Mom still sounded annoyed. "Clean up this mess and I'll set a mouse trap tomorrow."

Hannah stayed quiet. I knew she didn't

think the thumping and rattling had come from a mouse.

I couldn't stop grinning. This was great fun. Plus, Hannah deserved it.

"That's for the bad haircut, Hannah," I whispered to myself.

CHAPTER NINE

The next day was Saturday—the start of our weekend with Dad.

When I climbed out of bed, I suddenly felt nervous. What would Dad say when he saw my hair? What would Felicity say?

I bit my lip, staring into my closet and trying to decide what to wear. Finally, I decided not to worry. I put on my favorite pair of black jeans and a purple

T-shirt that said "Hey, Girl!" on the front. At least I would be comfortable.

When Dad and Felicity arrived, Hannah was in front of me. Dad hugged her first.

"Hey, Cassie girl!" Felicity said and patted my hair. "Look at you!"

By then, Dad had seen me.

"Cassie!" Dad said, and gave me a hug. "My beautiful little girl," he said. But he was frowning over my head at Mom.

"Surprise!" I said meekly. My face was burning.

"Why did you let her do that?" Dad asked Mom angrily.

Mom shrugged. "Ask the girls," she said, half smiling.

Dad looked at me. I gulped.

Dad looked around like he was deciding who to yell at.

But before he could say anything, Felicity said, "Let's go. I'm hungry."

Thank goodness for Felicity.

Felicity talked the whole way in the

car about how she had shaved her head when she was eighteen. I tried to imagine what Felicity would have looked like, but it was pretty hard. These days, she has fluffy brown hair that floats around her shoulders.

I could see Dad frowning while Felicity talked. He hated my hair. But I didn't feel sad like I thought I would. I felt annoyed. Why did I have to look like Dad wanted me to? Why couldn't I have really short hair if I wanted? Short hair didn't hurt anyone.

Hannah was scowling out the window, just like Dad.

I could see where she got it from.

When we sat down for dim sum, Felicity was still talking and Dad was still frowning.

I had just managed to choose a plate of pork dumplings from the cart when Dad finally said something.

"Did your mother let you cut your hair like that, Cassie?" Dad said. He said it like Mom had let me jump off a cliff.

I glanced at Hannah and bit into the soft dumpling. She looked white.

"Nope," I said, with my mouth full. Then I swallowed. "The hairdresser said it would suit me." That was true in a way.

"The hairdresser!" Dad looked around like he wanted to go and yell at the hairdresser.

Hannah was watching me with her mouth open. She still looked pale.

"But you're only nine years old!" Dad said, a little too loudly for a restaurant.

"So?" I yelled back. "I'm not a little girl anymore, Dad." I had heard those words somewhere before, but I couldn't think where.

Hannah was watching me closely now, half smiling.

Dad was turning red. But he didn't know what to say. My hair was already short, so what could he do? He took a gulp of tea.

Felicity saved the day. "Go, Cassie!" she said. "Fight for your rights, girl."

I like Felicity.

CHAPTER TEN

On Sunday night, we were back home and I was back in my secret hiding place.

Hannah was at her desk doing homework. I couldn't see her, but I could hear her turning pages.

I felt really good. I didn't care what people thought of my hair anymore. And I wasn't scared of Hannah. Short hair made me feel like a different person.

I picked up an old sneaker from the bottom of Hannah's closet and threw it into Hannah's room. I couldn't throw very well because I could only move my wrist, but I heard it thump on the carpet.

Right away, I heard Hannah gasp.

I leaned back into the wall, but I couldn't hear anything.

Then I heard Hannah stand up. I could hear her breathing quickly, as she crouched on the end of her bed, facing the closet.

I thought quickly. This was it. Time for the real fun.

I moved my feet to get balanced, then I thumped my hip against the side of Hannah's closet.

Thud.

Hannah gasped again and crawled backwards to the top of her bed.

I did it again.

Thud.

Then, I let out a growl from the back of my throat, "Grrrrrrruuuugh. . . ."

I saw the bed move as Hannah climbed off. I couldn't see her now, but I heard her bedroom door open.

Where was she going?

Suddenly, the light turned on in my bedroom. Hannah was checking my room! Clever Hannah.

I pushed back into the wall, trying to be as small as possible. The gap into my bedroom was right near my shoulder and my closet door was open. She would notice me for sure.

I couldn't see Hannah, but I could hear her breathing as she looked in my closet.

I stayed very still.

This was it.

Hannah was about to catch me.

I waited for Hannah to say something. But she didn't. Instead, she turned out my bedroom light, and was gone. I heard the hall door open and then shut.

I breathed out and leaned against the wall. I couldn't believe Hannah hadn't seen my shoulder through the gap.

I slipped out of the hiding spot and spent a few minutes in the bathroom. Then I went to find Hannah.

She was sitting in the living room. She was very still. Her face was white and her eyes were big. Then she saw me.

"Where have you been?" Hannah asked, but she sounded glad to see me.

"In the bathroom," I said. I wasn't sure if she'd believe me, but I switched on the TV and sat in the best chair.

Hannah nodded and tried to smile.

"Shouldn't you be doing your home-work?" I said. I tried to sound normal, but I wasn't used to talking to Hannah anymore.

Hannah nodded again.

"I think I'll do it out here," she said. But she didn't go and get her homework. She didn't move.

I pretended to watch TV, but my mind was racing. Hannah looked really scared. She had even forgotten not to talk to me.

I sat there, feeling a bit bad. I hadn't meant to scare Hannah this much. I just wanted to annoy her. I always thought she would figure out it was me. I just wanted

her to stop ignoring me. That was all.
Suddenly, it had all gone too far.

CHAPTER ELEVEN

The next morning, Hannah's face was pale and there were dark patches under her eyes. She didn't look like she had slept very well.

When we were leaving for school, Hannah said, "Cassie, do you ever hear things in your closet?"

"Like what?" I said. I didn't know what else to say.

"Like, um, banging?" Hannah looked at me sideways.

I shrugged, but I felt bad. Should I tell Hannah it was me? I didn't want her to stop talking to me again.

"No," I said, feeling guilty.

Hannah frowned down at her feet as she walked.

"It's probably nothing," I said hopefully.

That was it. I decided to stop knocking in the closet. No more games. Then Hannah would stop being scared. And if she never knew it was me in the wall, she would keep talking to me.

Perfect.

But the next morning, Hannah looked even worse. I had stopped banging, but Hannah was still scared.

At breakfast on the third morning, Hannah was so tired she looked sick.

Mom kept frowning as she watched Hannah. But Hannah was too tired to notice us watching her. She buttered a piece of toast and tried to cut it with her knife upside down. Hannah looked down at her knife as though she didn't understand why it wasn't cutting.

"Hannah, are you OK?" Mom said.

Hannah nodded and picked up her whole piece of toast to eat.

"Maybe you should stay home today,"

Mom said. "Get some rest in bed."

"Bed? No." Hannah looked scared. "I'm OK, Mom."

She put down the toast after one bite.

On the way to school, I felt like I had to look after Hannah rather than the other way around. I steered her around some dog poo on the sidewalk. She would have stepped in it for sure. I checked for cars as we crossed the road.

When we made it to my school, I watched Hannah walk slowly towards the high school. When would Hannah stop feeling frightened?

I had stopped banging days ago. Why was she still scared?

That night, I lay in bed worrying about Hannah. It was late, but Hannah had only just gone to bed.

I wished I could help Hannah without making her angry with me.

After a while, I climbed out of bed and slid into my secret spot. I wanted to check on Hannah.

It was completely dark and quiet. I listened carefully. Was Hannah asleep?

I could just barely hear Hannah sobbing in her bed. She wasn't sleeping, she was crying!

I had to tell Hannah the truth.

Even if she stopped talking to me again, I had to tell her. Anything was better than this.

I slipped out of the secret spot and went to Hannah's bedroom door. But I didn't knock. I didn't want to scare her even more.

"Hannah," I said. "Are you awake?"

I heard her sniffing and sitting up in bed, but she didn't turn on the light.

"Are you OK?" I asked as I walked into Hannah's room.

Suddenly, Hannah started crying hard.

"I'm so scared," she said between sobs.

I reached over and hugged her. But now Hannah was crying harder—deep, painful sobs that shook her whole body.

"It's OK, Hannah," I said. "Don't be scared." I curled her hair behind her ears.

"There's nothing to be scared of," I said. But Hannah kept sobbing as though she hadn't heard me. I had to calm her down.

"Come into my room," I said. "You can sleep with me in my bed."

That helped.

"OK," said Hannah between sobs. "But don't tell Mom."

"OK," I whispered. I picked up Hannah's pillow and took her hand. I led her into my bedroom.

Once I told Hannah what I'd done, she wouldn't talk to me for a very long time.

CHAPTER TWELVE

I put Hannah's pillow on the end of my bed and we both snuggled in with our heads on the two ends. I'm so short that there was still a lot of room.

Hannah had stopped crying now. She rested her legs against mine, as though she was glad to be touching someone. It felt good.

"Hannah," I said quietly. This was going to be hard.

But I didn't get a chance to say anything.

"I'm sorry I cut your hair," Hannah said in the dark. Her voice sounded clear and calm.

"That's OK," I said quietly. But I still didn't understand. "Why did you do it, Hannah?" I asked.

"I didn't mean to," Hannah said. "It was an accident. I didn't think about what would happen when I cut off your pigtail."

I was stunned. "You mean it really was an accident?" I said.

"Yeah. Sorry."

My mind raced. Hannah has always

been bigger than me, better than me, smarter than me. I never even imagined that she made mistakes.

"You mean, you didn't plan to cut it like that?" I said.

"Nope." Hannah sounded like she was smiling. "But it looks OK, don't you think?"

"But why did you stop talking to me?" I said. "If it was a mistake, why did you blame me?"

"Blame you? You blamed me!" Hannah said. "Did *you* know what would happen if I cut off a pigtail?"

I didn't say anything. I'd had no idea.

"You didn't know either, did you?"

Hannah said. "We didn't realize how short some pieces would be."

Hannah moved her legs away from mine.

"But I'm the one who got yelled at. Just because I'm older, I'm not allowed to make a mistake."

I stayed quiet, thinking.

"And then you started crying and yelling," Hannah went on. "You just acted like a baby again, and Mom felt sorry for you. I hate that."

Was it my fault, too? Was I blaming Hannah all this time, when it was partly my fault, too?

We were both quiet. I thought about the day Hannah had cut my hair. It seemed

like a long time ago—when I still felt like a little girl.

Hannah moved her legs back to touch mine. She didn't seem angry anymore.

"Why didn't you tell Dad what happened?" Hannah asked quietly.

I sighed. "I don't know," I said. "It has

nothing to do with Dad. It's between you and me."

"He was so angry!" Hannah giggled.

I giggled, too.

Now it all seemed really silly.

"Yeah, thank goodness for Felicity," I said.

That did it. Now we were really laughing.

"THANK GOODNESS for Felicity!" Hannah repeated in a funny voice, trying not to laugh too hard.

After that, we giggled and talked and tried to stay quiet until we fell asleep.

It turned out to be a really good night.

CHAPTER THIRTEEN

For the next few nights, Hannah sneaked into bed with me. She stopped looking so scared and she started sleeping well. She started talking to me again, too.

Hannah even helped me fix up my room. She offered me a poster of Orlando Towner to put up on the wall, but I said no thanks. I don't like Orlando Towner.

In the end, I put up a poster of Kayla

Storm. Maybe I'll try to grow my hair to look like her, too.

Hannah helped me pack away all the teddy bears and dolls. She was about to throw them in my closet, but I told her that a messy closet was bad luck.

Hannah looked at me strangely when I said that.

I never told Hannah about the secret spot or what I'd done. It doesn't seem to matter anymore. And Hannah never told me that she believes in ghosts. But we talk about lots of other things.

These days, Hannah still sneaks into my bed some nights. But I don't think she's scared anymore. I think she sleeps in my bed when she wants to talk.

Hannah told me about Josh, who plays the clarinet in the school band. And I told her about Sam, even though there's not much to tell.

Hannah doesn't hate me anymore. I'm not sure exactly when she changed her mind. Maybe it was me that changed. I don't just mean my hair—these days I never feel like a little girl, I just feel like me.

THE END

When faced with a mean new girl, will she be a good friend or be mean, too?

GO GIRL!

THE NEW GIRL

BY ROWAN McAULEY

Keep reading for an excerpt!

CHAPTER *ONE

One Wednesday morning in the middle of the year, a new girl arrived at Zoe's school. It was the most exciting thing that Zoe could remember happening for ages.

Ms. Kyle knocked on the door during class. Mr. Mack had to stop halfway through a sentence.

Everyone looked up from their books.

"Don't mind us," said Ms. Kyle. "I'm just

talking to Mr. Mack about the new student."

"Wow! A new student," Zoe whispered to her best friend, Iris.

"I know," said Iris. "And what perfect timing. Mr. Mack was speaking way too fast for me to keep up. Quick—while he's still talking to Ms. Kyle—are there two g's in *exaggerated*?"

"Shh," said Zoe. "I'm trying to listen."

But all around her the quiet whispers of the other kids were growing into loud mumblings. She couldn't hear what Ms. Kyle was saying at all.

"Settle down," said Mr. Mack, as Ms. Kyle left. "All right, you all heard that we're getting a new member of our class. Her name is

Isabelle Sinclair, and she will be joining us as soon as she's finished picking up her books and uniform at the office. I know you'll all do your best to make her feel welcome."

Definitely, thought Zoe. *Iris and I will be her best friends.*

"Ok, then," said Mr. Mack. "Let's get back to our vocabulary."

Of course, it was impossible for Zoe to concentrate on her schoolwork. Any minute now, Isabelle could walk through the door. . . .

Zoe wondered what Isabelle would be like. Would she be musical like Iris, funny like Ching Ching, brainy like Chloe, or shy like Olivia?

When Zoe had finished her vocabulary she started drawing little cartoons in the margins of her exercise book. She doodled all the different ways she thought Isabelle might look. Would she be tall or short? Would she have long hair, or—

long hair

short hair

curly hair

"Zoe!" Iris nudged her sharply in the ribs.

Zoe looked up and saw Mr. Mack looking at her pointedly.

"Nice of you to rejoin us, Zoe," he said, dryly.

Zoe quickly sat up straight and covered her drawings with her hand.

"Sorry, Mr. Mack," she said.

Mr. Mack was just about to say something else when there was a knock at the door. It was Ms. Kyle again, followed by a girl in a new school sweater.

Isabelle!

CHAPTER TWO

Isabelle Sinclair stood at the front of the classroom, looking coolly at her new classmates.

I'd be terrified if that were me, thought Zoe. *I'd be shivering all over.*

But Isabelle looked totally relaxed, even bored.

Ms. Kyle left the room and Mr. Mack turned to Isabelle.

"Well, Isabelle," he said, cheerily. "Welcome to our class. Would you like to tell us a little bit about yourself?"

Oh, no, Mr. Mack! thought Zoe, dismayed. *Don't do that to her!*

Zoe couldn't imagine anything worse on the first day at a new school. She wouldn't have known what to say, and she would have blushed and stammered. But Isabelle spoke confidently.

"My family just moved here because my dad got a transfer at work. He's a lawyer and my mom's a piano teacher. I don't have any brothers or sisters, but I have a weiner dog named Banger who sleeps on my bed."

"Thank you, Isabelle. It's good to have you here," said Mr. Mack. "Why don't you sit at that desk today, and we'll find you a permanent place tomorrow?"

He pointed to Lily's desk.

She was out sick.

The bell rang loudly for lunch, and before Mr. Mack could say another word, everyone had leapt to their feet.

"All right," he called out. "Off you go! Just remember to give Isabelle room to breathe, and time to eat her lunch, while you're busy mobbing her with questions."

Mr. Mack was right—the class *did* mob Isabelle. Everyone wanted to talk to her, be spoken to by her, find out more about her, and tell her about themselves.

"See that mulberry tree over there?" asked Oscar. "That's where Dylan and I climbed out over the school fence."

"We got in the worst trouble," said Dylan, grinning. "They made up a whole new school rule just for us. Now no one is allowed to climb trees."

"And the back of that building is the music room," said Iris, pointing. "We have guitars, a piano, a drum set, and flutes, and everything."

"And next to the music room is the

computer room," said Ching Ching. "We have computer class on Fridays with Mr. Campbell. He's a really good teacher."

Olivia giggled. "You would say that!" she said to Ching Ching. "You've got the biggest crush on him!"

"I so do *not*," said Ching Ching.

"You so do *so*," said Olivia, laughing. "You lo-oo-ove him!"

Go Girl!

If you loved this story, don't miss the rest of the series!

The new GIRL
BY ROWAN McAULEY

SLEEP-OVER!
BY ROWAN McAULEY

Dancing Queen
BY THALIA KALKIPSAKIS

Sister Spirit
BY THALIA KALKIPSAKIS

The WORST Gymnast
BY THALIA KALKIPSAKIS

Lunchtime Rules
BY VICKI STEGGALL